MOLLY WYER studied creative writing at Royal Holloway, College, University of London. She has written, edited and made tea for a variety of nonprofit organizations. She lives in San Luis Obispo, California. This is her second novel.

MATTHEW CARVER adapted the cover design of this book.

To Crystal —

Molly Wyer.

Californienne

by

Molly Wyer

ISBN 9780936315553
STARHAVEN, 42 Frognal, London NW3 6AG
books@starhaven.org.uk
https://starhavenpress.wordpress.com/
https://www.facebook.com/starhaven.org.uk/

Typeset in Palatino Linotype

To my grandmother, Winifred Ellis McKellar Wyer

a life lived with courage, grace and love

One must learn to love, and go through a good deal of suffering to get to it, and the journey is always towards the other soul.

– D. H. Lawrence

Here is the quiet light, the silent shore
Beyond the foaming world; here is the chart
Of the last journey, past the last desire.

– Joy Davidman

Prologue

Sandro Botticelli
'La Nascita di Venere'

I.

'La Nascita di Venere', 'The Birth of Venus'. So the placard read. Venus stood poised on the edge of her scallop shell, gazing out of the frame in a trance. One hand ineffectually covered her breasts, while the other used her long hair to cover her loins (with more success). The red-gold of her hair glinted, struck by sunlight, and her skin shimmered like pearls. Though she was caught in the act of covering herself, she did not seem in the least embarrassed by her exposure.

Ada tilted her head to one side. What was it about the face of Venus that drew one so? She had a secret – Ada could almost decipher it in her sea-green eyes and the delicate curve of her mouth.

"Ada!" She started at Mother's voice – it would not do to be caught staring so long at a nude.

II.

You could almost smell the sea spray, taste the salt in the wind blown by Zephyr as he directed Venus' shell ashore at Cyprus. When you first looked at her face, Venus seemed bashful, but then you looked a second time and realized that the painter had simply caught her deep in contemplation.

Who had the artist's model been? Jean blushed at the thought of posing for such a portrait. The way the artist had captured Venus' every curve, her intimate glance, spoke of a knowledge akin to that elusive thing called love. Fitting that the goddess of love was as mysterious as the thing itself. Plenty of boys were happy to spout that word, but none had yet propounded love's meaning to Jean satisfactorily.

III.

Beautiful things take time, and beautiful things deserve time. Beatrice stood in front of the painting for a long while, both in tribute to its beauty and in an effort to burn it into her memory, to absorb the mysterious loveliness of it. It felt a little strange to stare so long at a depiction of a naked woman, but while there was a sensuous glory to the painting, it was not sensual. Venus both invited the observer in and held one at a distance with her chaste, downcast gaze.

Beatrice moved on to admire the 'Primavera', but minutes later found herself back in front of the 'Venus'. At age twenty, due perhaps to a stubborn resistance to unpleasant facts, Beatrice knew only the sweet sting of unrequited devotion. But here, nearly evading her, yet hovering around the corners of Venus' mouth and eyes, she glimpsed intimations of something far more real – almost holy.

Another visitor came and stood beside her, and Beatrice realized that Mother and her brother had long since moved to another room in the massive Uffizi Gallery. She turned to go, hoping one day she and Venus would meet again.

I.

Ada

The photographer positioned her in the midst of a bower of chrysanthemums, orange blossom and lilies of the valley. It occurred to Ada, sitting in the parlor at The Laurels, momentarily without the buzzing of bridesmaids, that the room exuded the oppressive excess of fragrance and flowers that a funeral would have. The fancy made her shiver, but she composed her face again to look sweet for the camera.

Inexplicably, she thought of her mother's perfunctory advice that morning as Ada was being dressed in bridal white. Mother had stood behind her, hooking buttons on the bodice of the dress and relating the offices of the wedding night. Ada's cheeks flamed at the recollection, not least because the talk had awoken memories of June nights the previous summer, leaning up against walls on narrow, cobbled Florence streets, her breath catching when he held her to him the way it had caught when she had seen the Botticelli 'Venus' for the first time. Would it be the same between her and Harry? They had hardly had a moment apart from a chaperone in which to feel a flicker of passion since they had begun courting nine months ago.

They arrived back from eight weeks' honeymoon and settled into the cottage at The Laurels while they waited for a suitable house to become available. Ada was not sure what Mother meant by terms such as a "suitable house". The cottage would have been eminently suitable for a young couple in love, but now that Ada was quite sure that that was not the condition of Mr. and Mrs. Henry Campbell, the "character" and "charm" of the cottage – its many nooks and small wood-burning stove that was the only real source of heat – were irksome. No matter how grand and in-all-ways-suitable a house they might move into, she knew she would manage to find fault with it now, for love would not be there.

In the end, the house that they found was within walking distance of Harry's practice, and still an easy drive from The Laurels. With Mother's assiduity they soon had competent help and tasteful furniture. Days followed in which Ada arose, ate breakfast in silence with her husband while he read the newspaper and tilted her cheek so he could peck it as he walked out the door. That was that. Her existence as a tasteful furnishing in his life had begun. When he desired a particular meal, she was there to speak to Cook. When he needed a woman on his arm at social events to make a pleasant comment or to listen raptly to what he or another man said, he took her. When – not *very* often – he wanted a woman's body for his pleasure, he had but to reach for her.

It wasn't long before Mother began asking, with a meaningful smile, if Ada felt "quite well". Ada watched herself too, mockingly at times and almost as though she were somebody else, as she looked each month for signs. Perhaps she still cherished a hope that Harry would wake up and love her after she had produced his offspring, but equally she hoped that a baby would provide respite from his appallingly dull love-making.

Then came the morning when her corset felt too tight and her breasts seemed to spill over the top of it. Could it be... or was she just getting plump? (An ever-present danger Mother warned her against frequently.) Ada had been anticipating this event for months and knew the pain of convincing herself that she was with child, only to be proven wrong days later by the hated red tide. So she watched for further signs and wore her corset a little less snugly.

Faintness came next. One minute she was standing in Elena's studio, admiring her sister's foray into portraiture – a painting of a young man whose likeness, at least, was very handsome – the next, she was fumbling for a space not covered in paints to sit down. She feared Elena's sharp eyes would catch her out, but they were still fixed on the portrait.

Next morning Ada awoke to a raging headache. She dared for once to stay upstairs and sent word for Cook to make up a tray of tea and dry toast and for Harry not to look for her at breakfast. She half expected him to fly into a rage and demand her presence, or else to come up and look in on her before he left. But the front door opened and closed promptly at his usual time, and she hid her disappointment behind a lavender-scented cloth draped over her eyes.

A week on, her cycle was later than it ever had been, yet she refused to acknowledge to herself that she might well be pregnant. Mother was hosting a tea at The Laurels in an effort to find Ada a worthy local charity to support. Among the attendees were to be a board member from Mother's home for the aged and an actress from the Pasadena Playhouse. It would be considered very *avant-garde* of Mother to invite a member of an acting troupe to tea.

As Ada brushed her hair, she wondered idly what would be on the menu. Egg salad perhaps, or smoked salmon sandwiches? Without warning, her stomach heaved at the thought of fish, and she scrambled for the toilet.

This could prove difficult. She stared at her sallow reflection in the mirror for several minutes more. Meeting ladies over tea whilst trying not to gag at the smell of – of... She ran for the toilet again.

In the event, Ada was late. Mother's forced smile from across the room said her absence had been noted. Thankfully, there were enough people circulating that Ada's presence could hardly have been missed. A pianist was playing "Maple Leaf Rag" on the old Steinway in the sitting-room and a selection of family curios was on display – mementos collected on travels; ample entertainment for their guests. Ada paused to adjust her hat and fan her flushed face prior to venturing into the fray. Elena bustled past on some errand, stopping to reassure her that there was no real need for her to be there till they sat down. Perhaps Elena had observed more in her studio than she had let on.

It was a lovely warm day for March, and tables had been set up on the lawn on the north side of the house. Strains of a Mozart piano sonata now drifted out through the open French doors, along with servants carrying trays of sandwiches, bowls of chicken salad, baskets of fresh rolls, platters of blood oranges and hothouse strawberries... Suddenly Ada was ravenous.

She could barely attend to the garrulous woman to her left, whose girth made Ada suspect that it was she who had spearheaded the monthly bake sale for the church organ refurbishment fund. Finally, in an attempt to hear no more about Mrs. Owens's famously flaky liver and onion pie, Ada turned to the woman on her right – the actress whom Mother had invited on a whim.

She seemed out of place, with her dark-eyed, glamorous beauty, amidst an array of women mostly of middle age and all but a few of "a certain background". Many of them looked askance at The Actress now and then, though commenting to each other in whispers that of course it was "very good" of Mrs. Thomas to have invited a representative of the local dramatic society. They seemed to have adopted, wholesale, the prejudice of a previous generation that all actors were dissolute libertines, not to be associated with – certainly not to be numbered among "polite company".

Partly on principle, therefore, but mainly out of necessity, Ada introduced herself.

"I'm Eve," the woman said, in a deep voice that set Ada to musing what a fine Cleopatra she would make.

At that moment, salmon sandwiches passed in front of them, and Ada recoiled involuntarily.

Eve quirked a well-defined eyebrow.

Ada felt compelled to give an explanation. "I'm a bit tired, and sometimes that makes me particular about smells." Even as she said it, almost defiantly, Ada knew how unconvincing it sounded. Better to have said nothing! But Eve merely smiled and waved a servant over.

"A glass of red wine for Mrs. Campbell," she said; then, leaning over, she added in a confidential whisper, "I find a little wine generally cures most kinds of sickness – though if it's the nine-month's kind, you may find yourself..."

Eve must have caught a flash of panic in Ada's glance to either side, for she laughed and finished by saying, "Never fear, your secret is safe with me. Though why a married woman need keep it a secret is, I admit, quite intriguing!"

She tilted her head as Ada began to marshal her proofs of not being "in the family way". Suddenly she was too tired to keep on with the ruse. And it would be such a relief to tell *someone*. Regardless, that glass of wine looked surprisingly good, and rare indeed was the occasion when Mother allowed her a glass, even for medicinal purposes. As for Harry – he refused to consider wine a reasonable budget item, though he was not opposed to drinking it at someone else's expense.

Smiling weakly, Ada took a sip of the jewel-toned liquor.

"Now tell me everything," Eve whispered, leaning closer in her daringly-cut gown. It was indeed a gown, and would have looked preposterous on anyone else at an afternoon tea. On her it looked regal and perfectly suited to the occasion.

Ada realized Eve's eyes were still fixed on her. She gazed back blankly.

"Well? The story! There must be something salacious going on for you to be so secretive."

Ada sighed. "Wouldn't that be nice?" She blushed at having expressed such a thought aloud, but Eve threw back her head and laughed.

"Darling, I hardly know you, and already I adore you." She laid a hand on Ada's arm. "And I'm longing to hear your pedestrian tale more than ever."

Ada took another sip of wine and launched into an only slightly embellished account of her domestic woes. The breeze tugged at her hair, and she paused a moment to secure her hat with a pin. She was aware once again of her surroundings: the lavish March sun, the verdant lawn in such contrast to the white appliqué lace tablecloth and its bowls of pink roses, the thrum of conversation and click of china...

She was also aware of what she did not feel: she didn't feel ill anymore. Either the glass of wine, or the relative novelty of a new and stimulating conversation partner had at last cured her of her misery – for the time being. She turned again to Eve – Miss Haskins, rather – but at that moment, someone tapped Ada on the shoulder.

She looked around to see Mother behind her chair, smiling serenely but looking all the same deeply determined.

"Please excuse me, my dear," Mother said to Eve, "but I must introduce my daughter to some of our other guests, or they will be *so* disappointed."

Ada rose slowly, more from a desire not to reawaken her sickness than from stubbornness, and followed her mother.

Between introductions – "Mrs. Sewell, who runs the orphans' charity gala; her husband is in oil", "Mrs. Travers, who is on the committee for the fine arts; her husband is in politics, you know" – Mother remonstrated with Ada for her tardiness. "And why must you give all your time to the one guest who is likely to prove controversial? And drinking wine – at three in the afternoon? I know young people are less concerned about such things, but it isn't appropriate at all for a tea, you know, and several ladies here are on the temperance committee! What on earth – "

"You may tell them, if they ask, that I was feeling ill."

Mother opened her mouth to protest.

"It's true." Ada wondered if she ought to tell Mother of her suspicion. But damn it all if she would allow a few cantankerous women to dictate her life down to the tiniest detail! It was miserable enough without their interference. "I felt unwell and Miss Haskins ordered me a glass of wine. And I will say –" she plowed on before Mother could add objections, "that it worked like a charm. I feel fine now!" And, smiling in a way she knew was unbearably smug, Ada returned to her seat.

Her jubilant mood was short-lived. Miss Haskins had to leave for rehearsal. She promised to visit Ada soon, however, and even suggested that her new friend come to take a seat at the dress rehearsal of their troupe's play.

The woman who sidled over to take Eve's place was so assured of her own superiority to "fallen women", which she claimed that her institution helped, that Ada marveled there were any who could stomach her charity. Then again, most of those women likely had no choice.

At length, mercifully, the guests departed. Mother went indoors to supervise clearing up, and Ada wandered to her favorite childhood retreat – the sunken garden. Settling in the late afternoon sun, she watched shadows process from the stables up towards the house. Tucked away here, she could observe the whole world going past – at least, it had felt like a whole world to her in the years before she had been sent off to The Bishop's School.

To Ada's surprise, she now saw Elena coming from the direction of her studio, arm in arm with a man. He looked familiar, and after a moment Ada recognized him as the man in the portrait Elena had recently completed. The pair paused behind a hedge that shielded them from all eyes save Ada's, and she nearly jumped up shouting as the man, dressed in *stable livery*, put his hands on Elena's hips and began kissing her. Outrage swiftly modulated to a different key as Ada realized that Elena was welcoming his advances. She would have to have a word with her sister! But then... another thought struck her like a chill night breeze. Not once had Harry touched her with such desire.

Ada could feel her face heating by degrees as she watched, until finally the intimacy of the scene overwhelmed her and she awoke to the impropriety of observing it. She sought to regain the tranquility of the solitude she'd been basking in a short time before, but it was gone. In its place was an unbearable ache, as of loss. She remembered again summer twilights along the Arno, but even those images seemed washed out in the light of what she'd just witnessed.

Ada flitted about, rearranging a book here, plumping a pillow there, then doing it all over again. If Harry were here, he would admonish her for allowing her nerves to govern her – but, thankfully, he was at his practice.

She poked her head into the kitchen to check on the progress of sandwiches and cake, but Cook was (as ever) one step ahead of her and had Lily helping to arrange the various items on trays. Catching a whiff of egg salad, along with Cook's calm, what-are-you-doing-here stare, Ada fled.

She moved to the entryway and, inspecting a large bouquet in the center of the room, withdrew and replaced a few sprigs of foliage at random. Hearing tires grinding on gravel, she hurried back to the sitting room to await her guest's arrival with what composure she could muster.

Eve breezed in before she could be announced and took both of Ada's hands. Ada's thoughts of decorum and creating the right impression instantly melted away.

"My dear, you must tell me all your face cream and rouge secrets! You look like the dew of the morning is yours! Or is it as I suspected – that you have a," Eve dropped her voice as Ada's hands jerked convulsively, "a little passenger?"

Ada swallowed, and Eve collapsed gracefully into a nearby armchair. "Mmm," her wide, expressive mouth curved up in a faint smile. "Well then, perhaps we ought to start our conversation with something less – fraught? Here! I brought you my favorite macarons – from that little French confectioner's in Grand Central Market."

She handed Ada a shallow ivory box, tied with black satin ribbon. Within reposed a rainbow of delectable-looking confections, the like of which Ada had never seen outside of France. Ada smiled and they settled down to chat.

"I sometimes dream of running off and joining a convent – even though none of our family is Catholic." Ada glanced down. "I don't suppose they'd take me now, anyway."

"Don't be melodramatic, darling. You must leave that to us professionals." Eve studied her new friend from behind a teacup. "Besides, I predict you will not always find a life of chastity so appealing as you do now."

Ada felt her cheeks flame and looked toward the door, though no one was there. Eve always spoke in a discrete tone, but... Ada tried to compose her features into an admonitory expression, but Eve merely quirked one lip and said,

"So when are you going to tell your family about it?" nodding at Ada's stomach, which Ada shielded instinctively.

"When I'm sure." – She could hear obstinance in her tone.

"Oh, and when will that be? When your child is suckling at your breast?" – Eve shrugged off Ada's anguished glance at the doorway this time. "Your cook is clearly very capable, but your other help is either exceptionally discrete *or* adept at staying out of the way of potential work."

That point was difficult to argue. Still. Ada tried a new tack. "Tell me about your new play!" she inquired. "How is it coming along? When may I come see you at work?"

"A clever ruse, albeit a transparent one," Eve smiled. "Fortunately for you, I, like all truly great artists, have as great an ego, so I'll happily be diverted. We are making great progress on *Othello*, and I'm pleased to report that yours truly has been cast in the role of Desdemona. She's a bit weak-kneed for my taste, but the man they've cast for Othello is – *well*, he can send shivers down your spine just by looking at you, and I don't intend merely to be looked at." – Eve drew a long, slow breath. "So, I suppose I won't mind playing the much-wronged wife *just* this once."

Ada felt both embarrassed and exhilarated. No woman had spoken of a man so in her hearing before, though she'd certainly overheard far more explicit commentary on "the fairer sex" from her father's business associates when they'd believed none of the family was within earshot. They confined themselves generally to women they did not consider "ladies," but on a few occasions she'd discovered herself to be the brunt of their comments.

One vile coal magnate had, in a memory which Ada had, till this moment, successfully buried, grabbed the back of her dress, and what was beneath, as she had attempted to hurry indoors one night at The Laurels. He had been smoking a cigar in the deep, jasmine-hung shadows of the patio, and she, coming home from an evening of bridge with Harry (bridge had featured prominently in their courtship), had not spotted him there until the last moment. By the time she'd caught a waft of smoke and seen the cigar's point of light and a dark shape behind it, it was too late for good manners to turn her back. He had of course already seen her.

Experience of her father's business guests suggested that she not linger long with one alone – they all seemed given to familiarities once they were in liquor – so she moved quickly past the coal magnate towards the open doors. She was nearly breathing a sigh of relief when she felt the pressure of his hand on her from behind, squeezing and feeling as though she were a thing that belonged to him.

Her mind had numbed and all she could think of was that she must get in, and so she'd kept walking, never making a sound or looking back. That was what she hated most about the memory now. It still made her feel voiceless – wanting to scream but unable to force out a sound.

She'd had to face him at breakfast the next morning, pretending for someone's sake – her own or her father's? – that none of it had happened, or at least been remembered, and that the faint whiff of cigar smoke on his jacket when he entered the breakfast room didn't make her gag.

A hand on her arm recalled her to the present.

"I am so sorry, I –" Ada felt her eyes filling with unexpected tears and took a hasty gulp of tea to quell them.

"Don't apologize, my dear. *I* make it a rule never to apologize for being myself!"

Conversation progressed to other topics and Ada wondered how Eve could already feel like an old friend – though no friend from her past, not even the most daring of the Bishop's girls, had flouted the expectations of polite society so much on principle as Eve seemed to do.

Before they knew it, two hours had fled, and Eve had to make a hasty departure for a costume fitting. As she watched her whip her glossy red roadster round the drive and speed off down the street, Ada felt a sense of melancholy settling over her. Before encountering Eve, she had not known how lonely she was in her new life, and so it had hurt less than it did now as she envisioned another dreary afternoon of embroidery and going over the weekly menu with Cook, then making light conversation with Harry over dinner...

The day came, only a week or so later, when Mother remarked: "You're looking very fresh and full-cheeked, Ada." Which, being translated, meant: "Ought you really to be taking a second helping of cake?"

To her consternation, Ada burst into tears, the forkful of cake in her mouth notwithstanding. Mother blinked for a second, then summoned a servant for a glass of cordial.

She pressed a handkerchief into Ada's hand: "Do you think, my child, that you may be in the family way at last?"

Ada bit her lip to imprison a vicious retort. Why on earth did people insist upon these roundabout expressions for something that was the sole method for the continuation of the human race?

*

Though the grand building was now a few years old, it still retained some scents of newness – fresh paint, fresh grout, wood sap. They crossed a magnificent mosaic floor, lit from above by natural light filtering down through a rotunda's massive skylight.

Ada could almost imagine herself back in Europe. The chill of marble was welcome after the heat outside, as was the cathedral-like stillness after a hectic drive through the city.

Not yet rich in its own collections (though the Los Angeles Fine Arts League, of which Mother was a member, was doing its best to remedy that), the museum hosted rotating art exhibitions; and when Eve had discovered there was a William Blake exhibit on, she had been adamant that they go *at once*. Now, pacing slowly around the walls covered in small and midsized prints, Ada could see why.

There was a mystical quality to the British poet/artist's work that seized the imagination as well as the senses. Ada paused in front of a print from his *Songs of Experience*: two girls knelt by a priest in a gazebo or garden. The poem's title, "The Garden of Love," came as a surprise to her, but she was even more astonished at its terse, combative verses.

"'Binding with briars my joys and desires'," Eve quoted, walking over to where Ada stood. A chill ran along Ada's spine at the pathos in her friend's tone; she glanced back at her, but Eve's face was a closed book. If Ada had been drilled in anything, it was above all not to ask invasive questions. She tucked the moment away in her mind and moved to a nearby print, "Beatrice Addressing Dante from the Car".

"Well, that was both lovely and enlightening. And now, I think, I could use a pick-me-up. So could you, by the look of you!" Eve linked arms with Ada and hummed "I Didn't Raise My Boy to Be a Soldier" as they went to retrieve her car.

Late afternoon sunlight fluctuated between pleasant and oppressive as they drove. At length, Eve drew up to a curb by an establishment proclaiming itself The Golden Sun Saloon.

"What is it, darling? You look like someone just walked over your grave! Don't you like this place?"

"That's just – oh no! I mean, I've never been in a saloon before, even with a man, let alone without one." Ada summoned her resolve. "But I am fully prepared to change that. And I *am* dying for a drink!"

Laughing, they made their way in, and Eve steered them to a quiet booth. As her eyes adjusted from the brightness outside, Ada took in the cool and dark of her surroundings. Where The Golden Sun's walls were not bare brick, they were deep navy, and a long mahogany counter gleamed under glittering chandeliers. The wall behind the bar was lined with mirrors, doubling an extensive liquor collection.

Eve said something to the barman as they passed, and before Ada had time to wonder how and what one ordered in a saloon, two drinks appeared. At first glance they looked like champagne, and she felt a flash of disappointment as they chinked glasses. But as she took her first sip, a taste of berries made her look up in surprise.

"Nice, isn't it?"

She nodded.

"Kir Royale. Johnny knows it's my favorite. I thought you might like one too."

"It's beautiful." Ada held her glass up to the light, watching infinitesimal bubbles rise through gradations of magenta, blush and gold.

"Altogether pleasing to the senses," said Eve, taking another sip.

Ada did the same, and felt the fizz tickle her tongue and bloom on her palette...

"Isn't it amazing? It's quite the party trick when you think of it. They tell you how to dress, whom to marry and when, what charities are deserving of your time – what time isn't occupied with bearing and raising children, that is. And if you're tempted to question the rules, they threaten you with the specter of the Fallen Woman – destitute and unloved. All the while *they* are the very ones who shape society such that she remains a pariah." – Eve drew a breath and, laughing shakily, laid her hand on Ada's. "You must forgive me, my dear. Though I have long since fled the forces that bound me, the injustice of it all still smarts. Particularly when I see another such bird caught in the snare."

Their eyes held for a long moment, till Ada's misted over and she looked away.

A few weeks later, Ada received a letter from Eve:

Sometimes a madness takes one like a fever and the only way to cure it is to let it run its course. I have, in spite of myself, fallen in love with my Othello, and it is indeed a glorious madness! I feel as though I'd found the "wings of the morning" King David sang of those many thousand years ago.

You would not know it from his rather cold, stoic demeanor, my dear, but he is a deeply passionate man. I tremble like a schoolgirl just thinking of him. Alas! I can feel all my high-minded resolve to maintain my independence crumbling, and I will almost certainly marry him when he asks me.

You see? I do have it badly. Tomorrow we are taking a drive along the famous Ridge Route, which even such a keen motorist as I have yet to drive. He says he particularly wants to watch the sunset with me from the Sandberg's Summit Hotel. Could this be it? I know we are going at breakneck speed, but life is so fragile a thing I have no intention of slowing down for convention's sake.

Ada put the letter down and stared abstractedly out the window at the gardener, who was deadheading rosebushes.

There comes a time in every woman's life when she must not merely make her own decisions, but do so according to principles she is deeply persuaded by, rather than simply parroting those of her antecedents. This is complicated for her by the many within her family and her social sphere who hold the conviction that she'd much better let them, with their superior understanding of the world, of Holy Writ and of her personal affairs, decide her future for her. For that really is what it comes down to – a series of shaping decisions, little and big, that over time mold a life.

Ada had the feeling that she was nearing a conclusion from which there would be no retreat. Her palms began to sweat, and she was about to sit down, when the phone rang, and Lily announced, "Mrs. Thomas, Ma'am."

"Hello?"

"My dear, I hope you remember you have your fitting at the corset-maker this afternoon."

Ada swallowed. She had forgotten, not unintentionally. She knew she was measuring quite differently than she had on her last visit, and if all went well the change would only increase as the months progressed.

"Yes, Mother. I'll tell Mrs. Favel hello from you."

In the event, Mrs. Favel was an angel and made no comment on Ada's waistline; she merely noted down various widths and breadths in her little book.

As Ada was stepping back into the light out of the gentle gloom of the shop, a cloud passed over the sun and she had a sense of foreboding. The light soon returned, but her anxiety remained, and she put a hand to her stomach protectively.

She half-expected Eve to ring with news at some unholy hour of night, given the tone of her letter, but no call came. Ada told herself that either 'her Othello' had not proposed, or – quite likely – Eve had others to phone before a friend of only a couple months' acquaintance. Ada tried not to feel injured as she contemplated the second possibility.

She and Harry breakfasted as usual the following morning. Dry toast was now Ada's standard, but of this Harry seemed to take no notice. He ate his eggs and toast in his normal silence, shuffling through the paper.

"It looks like the weather will be fine again today." Ada smiled. After all, they had to raise this child together, presumably; one might as well try to maintain basic civility.

Harry grunted and turned a page. Ada gripped her teacup so hard she was surprised the handle didn't break. Well then, if silence was what he wanted...

As was her habit, she went to peruse the paper after he had finished with it. The sections were stacked on the sideboard in the reverse order to which he'd read them, so it was right at the end that she came to the *Extra* – something about a car crash near Deadman's Curve. Ada's wits were increasingly sluggish these days, and it was not until she was well into the article that she felt a surge of panic.

"... two motorists, both were thrown from the vehicle. The woman, leading lady of our local Playhouse, Eve Haskins, was declared dead..." The edges of the page blurred, and the sheet slipped from Ada's hand.

She clenched the arms of her chair and drew a shaky breath. She tried to force her mind to think some sensible thought, or at least to read the rest of the article, but she could not. She looked over at Harry for some kind of support – notice even – but he was sipping the dregs of his coffee and staring intently at nothing. Her stomach began to get that too-familiar seasick feeling and, standing, she made an unsteady way to the bathroom.

Ada emerged shaking still, but with a head clear enough to be outraged that her husband had not said a word to her about the accident. He had met Eve! Could he have failed to recognize that Ada and she had become devoted to each other over these months? Perhaps he really did not care, or was relieved at a prospect of no more intrusion by this particular friend? Ada let her mind run. So long as she could be angry, she could hold grief at bay.

*

What Ada loved most about winters in California was the wild, changeable light. Say, for instance, one was riding the train north of Santa Barbara: one minute you were flying through vineyards flaming gold against chill blue shadows, the next a ravine full of sycamores was catching fire as the sun slanted low across it. Then, as shadows deepened to purple, the sere mountains were bathed in a wash of pink –alpenglow that even the Swiss might envy.

This Christmas season, though, was one of the wettest she could remember, and today the sun had barely broken through roiling layers of cloud in the late afternoon. As the light waned, winds gusted more steadily, sending a few yellow leaves scurrying across the courtyard.

Ada lay on a daybed, propped on pillows, looking out the French windows at the violent weather. Inside, all was calm. Harry was at work; a fire crackled on the hearth; Tommy the Cat lay curled in a fat, shaggy ball. From the direction of the kitchen came faint rustlings as Cook made hot chocolate.

All was coziness and comfort, save for the large melon that had replaced Ada's stomach, and for the ominous pains in her lower back that suggested (so Mother informed her) that the passenger within would soon be making his or her debut.

Childbirth held an added terror for Ada ever since she had heard about Iona Brown's poor baby, who had died a few short weeks after birth. Mother had introduced Ada and Iona as two first-time mothers-to-be, though a friendship had not really ignited. Now, instead of cuddling a baby, poor Iona had to try to adhere to a slimming diet while her child lay in the churchyard.

Then, too, came all the ordinary pains and indignities that one's body suffered in bringing a life into the world. Ada's brother's wife Olive had been unsparing in acquainting her with these; perhaps it was as well, but it did little to dispel Ada's apprehensions. According to Olive, everyone exclaimed over Baby while the mother lay like a backdrop, expected to glow like a Madonna in a Titian painting, regardless of how chafed her breasts were, or how sore other parts of her or how much blood she was still losing.

A blast of wind carried golden leaves and a spatter of rain against the windows. A draft ran through the room; the fire spluttered in the grate, and Ada drifted to sleep.

She woke with an intake of breath. It was dark. The wind had risen to gale force, and the spattering rain had increased to a steady downpour. There was no light in the room save for the fire, which still snapped and cackled, and Tommy the Cat still lay cuddled up to its warmth. All was serene, and Ada wondered why she had awoken. Then a hand of fire twisted her stomach, and she knew. If only the pain would subside, she could get up and call... But then, as suddenly as it had come, it was gone, and she felt so sleepy that summoning help didn't seem important.

She woke again. Hours had passed. Or minutes – it did not matter. The pain was the only thing that mattered.

She must have cried out, because moments later, Cook came running, her be-floured apron still around her girth.

"The baby – " Ada panted as she held her middle and sweat pearled on her forehead.

She grasped Cook's hand. A fresh wave hit.

"I'll call Dr. Campbell's office and tell them he must come home straight away, Ma'am."

"Never mind Dr. Campbell." – The staff maintained the polite fiction that hers and Harry's was a loving relationship, but Ada was in no mood to play along when she could barely speak. "Have Philip bring the car around and tell Lily," she saw the maid now, leaning against the doorframe looking pale, "to finish packing my hospital bag."

Cook nodded at Lily, who disappeared with obvious relief. Then, with a squeeze of Ada's hand, Cook left to alert the chauffeur. She hurried back a minute later.

"He's bringing the car round, and as soon as your bag is ready, we'll bring you out. Ma'am," Cook added in after-thought. "I haven't been able to get through to The Laurels.

The line seems to be down. But I've spoken to your brother, who is on his way over there with the message."

Ada nodded. The words made sense, she knew, but she could not seem to focus her mind on them long enough to understand. Someone moments later helped her to the car, attempting at the same time (unsuccessfully) to shield her from the rain with an umbrella. But Ada did not mind the rain. It felt cool on her hot cheeks and forehead.

Settling back in the car, she began to shake, either from the wet or because her body was revolting against the ordeal it was beginning to undergo. As they sped through darkened streets, she felt each uneven surface in every nerve, even while her mind floated among disjoined thoughts. She tried to brace herself to avoid the worst jostling, but still she moaned at each bounce over a pothole.

"There, there," said a familiar voice, and Ada realized that she was not alone. An anonymous hand stroked hers – Ada started and might have pulled away, but then a contraction seized her and she squeezed the hand tightly.

"I'm sorry, Ma'am, I know I should have sent Lily with you, but she was so scared. Faints at the sight of blood, or a word about it practically. And I couldn't let you go alone."

In the light of a passing street lamp, Ada saw Cook's round Irish face, full of solicitude and practicality. Ada was amazed that she hadn't thought to demand that Cook come.

The car curved into the hospital grounds. Philip jumped out and opened the door. Just as she was stepping gingerly out of the car, Ada gasped: a rush of warm water was streaming down her legs. She'd heard about this, but did it have to happen in front of the chauffeur and a miscellany of hospital staff? But in another moment she was again past caring what anyone thought.

Pain continued to lash her as the wind lashed the palm trees outside of the hospital window. Through her own groans and the noise of the storm, Ada perceived voices – the confident, capable one of a nurse, then one of a man (her doctor?) and, after a time, her mother's. She did not hear Harry's voice, but she hadn't really expected him to be here. She certainly didn't *desire* his presence.

The room drifted in and out to the rhythm of her contractions. Sometimes she was in other rooms – the head-mistress's office at Bishop's School the time when she'd been caught sneaking back in after going to a dance with a college student; her father's study not so long ago, when she'd tried vainly to convince him that Elena ought to be allowed to see her horse trainer if he made her happy.

A stab of pain so intense Ada ground her teeth to keep from screaming…

She was back in a bedroom in Florence, its little balcony overlooking the Arno, the Ponte Vecchio and the hills above Fiesole on the far side of the river…

At some point, Mother was braiding her hair. What a relief to have the damp curls off her neck and out of her face.

Things began to get serious. Still her private nurse had not arrived from Los Angeles, and her doctor was off delivering another baby. Ada could tell they were all trying to be calm to keep her so, but such pretense only angered her. Just because she was *giving birth* to a child didn't mean she'd suddenly *become* one herself. Tears of vexation sprang to her eyes. Then the pain redoubled, and all other thoughts fled.

Harry appeared, looking equal parts concerned and disgruntled to be there. He vanished shortly after, and at long last her doctor appeared. He then vanished, and panic rose in Ada's breast. Another time-stopping contraction...

The next thing she knew, she was being wheeled into a delivery room and ordered to push. She was disinclined to obey, until her body took over and she had no choice.

It would never cease to amaze Ada how a single moment in time could be so transformative. One instant all was primal violence, her own body waging bloody war, the next peace and a pink little face beneath a thatch of nut-brown ringlets nuzzling at her breast. There was a murmur of voices in the background, then she and baby Regina Eve were transported to a room of their own with a view of the San Gabriel Mountains, newly flocked with snow.

Ada and baby Jean (it quickly became clear Regina would never stick) slept for a while, then Nurse – Ada's own nurse, who had finally made it through the storm – brought in a tray of eggs, toast and fresh orange juice. Everything tasted a thousand times better to Ada than it had a few hours before.

Mother came and kept her company. Through a haze of sleep Ada glimpsed Harry returning and inspecting little Jean, holding her to the light at the window, turning back a corner of the pink blanket in which she had been wrapped to expose her tiny, determined chin. Then he replaced Jean in her crib and explained to Mother (just outside the door) that he had to get back to his practice, and would she be able to stay with Ada a while longer? Of course, Mother agreed – she would just dash home for her needlework and a few necessaries... Ada drifted back to sleep, vaguely annoyed with herself for harboring a hope that this once, Harry might soften from automaton to human. – Would he have preferred a son? an heir? Looking at their daughter, Ada was reminded of a line, she supposed from the Bible, which suited the occasion perfectly: "She is better to thee than seven sons."

As Mother wrote letters and chatted about Elena's new horse, Ada nursed Jean again, wondering at the fierce vitality of such a little life.

Fairy lights twinkled on a small tree framed by the darkening window, and she remembered that it was almost Christmas. For a wonderful moment, there was a hush on the ward – a lull between labors – and outside all was calm; the storm had blown itself out at last. Ada looked down at her baby, once again drinking milk eagerly, eyes closed tight, and thought what it would be like to undergo the same ordeal she had just endured, but on straw and surrounded by the smell of stale animal sweat and manure. Cold, no doubt, and with only a bewildered husband twice your age to do what must be done; then, when it was over, the blood covered over with new hay, visitors arriving with a strange tale – shepherds, men, crowding the stable with talk of an army of singing angels; and Mary, too weary even to be perturbed at these intruders, looking with a mixture of awe and disbelief at the infant in her arms, falling asleep as He suckled at her breast...

Bob picked them up from Pasadena Hospital around half-past eleven, Ada protesting that her brother should not use his lunch break for her when a chauffeur would do just as well and Bob insisting that he loved to drive so much that it was never an imposition. He took the long way home, past the bulbous roots of the San Gabriel Mountains, and Ada decided there and then that, once she was well enough again, she would have him teach her to drive.

*

She came at last in sight of the sea. A weight lifted off her as she caught the familiar scent of salt and seaweed, saw the blues and greens shifting and glinting in the sun all the way to the horizon, felt that peculiar freshness that only comes with a breeze off the ocean.

Ada unpinned her hat and let the wind cool her head after a long hot drive. Leaving her car on the cliffs, she made her way down a sandy path to the beach. It was midday and mid-week, and nobody was about. She slipped off her shoes and stockings and felt the hot sand between her toes. When she got to the water's edge, she expected a shock from the cold, but it was wonderfully refreshing.

She waded in up to her calves. A wave surged close to shore and soaked a corner of her dress. She retreated with reluctance. As she returned to her belongings, Ada trod on something hard. Stooping down, she found a blush-and-white scallop shell still intact, buried in the sand. Her hair came loose from its bun and tumbled into her eyes, and she straightened in irritation. Then an idea seized her.

There was still no one but herself on this lonesome stretch of beach. She placed the shell carefully in one shoe, then slipped out of her dress, then her undergarments, till nothing but her hair shielded her from the sun. She felt so light as the breeze played about her that she almost fancied she might blow away. She waded back into the ocean.

Ada and Maisie stepped out of Ada's dusty car and stretched their limbs, cramped from the long drive. It had been dark on the way up to La Cuesta Encantada, but one could still get a sense of danger from the way the car had swayed around turns, blackness yawning to one side or the other. Just as they drew up, the moon had blown out from behind banks of cloud to cast a silver light on the road, the looming 'castle' above them and to the west, the sea.

"'Softly she was going up/And a star or two beside'," Ada murmured, words from Coleridge rising in her unbidden as she stood entranced by the moon's mellow light.

They waited, shivering, for only a few moments before the housekeeper came down lighted steps to greet them and a few broad-shouldered young men took their bags and disappeared. Their drive had started as well as ended in the dark, and Ada followed the housekeeper in an exhausted haze until they reached their rooms. Mr. Hearst's eccentric rules forbade late night supper in one's room, they were reminded, but Ada was too tired to eat, anyway.

She awoke to knocking on the door. Ada mumbled into her pillows ungraciously, but Maisie let herself in and began to pull open curtains and make an outrageous amount of noise, given her petite figure. Ada moaned. Maisie was one of Eve's set of theater friends, all of whom Ada's mother would have described as "fast"; yet once you got to know them, they were lovely. *They* hadn't given her the cold shoulder after the divorce. Quite the opposite. Besides, they too had loved Eve.

"Come, you don't want to miss breakfast! You know Mr. Hearst's house rules."

"Just another half-hour," Ada protested, but her stomach was starting to grumble.

She propped herself on her elbows and looked around. This was the first time she'd had a proper look at the room she'd been allotted. She was lying in an ornately carved four-poster bed that no doubt had lived another full life in a castle in Europe. A painting that hung beside the window across from her looked like a Renaissance Madonna and Child. No doubt it was. And that ceiling. It would all have seemed a bit much in another house, but Julia Morgan had designed this residence in such a way that it could just about hold all its artefacts with the grace they deserved.

Going to the window, Ada opened the casement and leaned out into cool morning air. The vista was of brown-sugar hills dotted with live oaks cascading down to where the ocean surged around San Simeon Point. Nearer to hand, roses, azaleas and palms grew lushly; and in the middle distance you could make out a herd of zebras.

After breakfast, learning that there were as yet no plans for one of Mr. Hearst's infamous horseback-riding excursions, Ada made her way to her favorite spot on the ranch: the Neptune Pool. The terrace that swept round the pool offered views of the crystalline Pacific on one hand and of the Santa Lucia Mountains rolling away into the distance on the other. If it was hot, the colonnades offered respite – and, of course, there was the pool itself. Ada had heard it described more than once before her first visit, but had still been awed upon seeing it. In a way, she still was – and to think a woman was its architect! Ada made her way to the changing rooms; it was a warm day for early May and she fancied a dip.

She plunged in and stroked across, trying to warm herself after the shock of cold water. She paused by a marble statue of Venus, staring. Nothing to compare to the Venus de Milo or – what felt more significant to her own life – the Botticelli Venus. No doubt 'The Birth of Venus' was resurfacing in her mind as Jean was now touring Europe with Ada's own mother and had written that they hoped to be in Florence "by the time this letter reached" her.

Ada dove into the cool depths again, trying to drown out a voice (her mother's? her own?) that said she ought to be the one taking Jean on her grand tour and talking to her about love – or perhaps primarily what love was not. She ought to be the one trying to help her to understand that, even when you loved someone a great deal, it was not always possible to give them what they needed, or wanted.

"Mind if I join you?"

Ada looked up to see a man gazing down at her from the pool's edge. He had a slightly canine smile; then again, perhaps that was in her head – after one or two abortive attempts at love since her failed marriage, Ada had come to regard all men as ravening wolves. Or at least she tried strenuously to warn herself off any handsome man when she encountered one, such as the one she was now nodding permission to – purely out of politeness, of course. Certainly it was nothing to do with the fact that he looked tanned and well-built in his bathing costume.

He slipped into the water without flinching. "Solomon." He smiled again, extending a hand.

She detected a faint foreign lilt to his voice but could not place it. After a moment, she realized in horror that he was still holding out his hand; in her preoccupation with his person and origins she had rudely ignored it. She grabbed it now too fervently, shaking it with both of her own. Surely her age and years of experience of the world had trained her better. She was acting as Jean had around young men the last time Ada had visited her in La Jolla. Dropping Solomon's hand, Ada moved quickly away after giving her name.

Sunlight fell on them like a warm gaze: personal, caressing. Ada did her best to appear unconcerned by his presence and taken up with her exercises.

Men were never to be trusted, she kept reminding herself every time Solomon – Mr. Leveson – appeared at her side: at cocktail hour that evening, two drinks in hand; at a wretched hour the next morning when Mr. Hearst summoned them all to join a riding trek, with a flask of coffee; again that evening to offer the loan of his bedroll, saying that it might provide some added cushion on the lumpy ground where Mr. Hearst had finally declared they would make camp.

"But what will you sleep on?" Ada wondered. "No. Thank you, I cannot accept." She wished her voice sounded firmer.

He smiled and shrugged.

She watched his retreating back, wondering what his design was, and how he managed to look so fresh at the end of a hot, dusty day of riding – and how to stop looking at shoulders she'd been confronted with in the pool a day before. She would have to avoid him altogether, to be safe.

Yet somehow, later that night, they were the last two people seated around the campfire, enjoying heat from the remaining embers and admiring a host of stars overhead. He did not try to say anything clever, or quote Keats's "Bright Star", and that pleased Ada. He seemed content to share in the awe and silence with her, which felt far more intimate than self-disclosure or poetry. In the end she was first to speak, afraid of the depths of knowing they were sinking into.

"Do you have children, Mr. Leveson?"

"Solomon, please," he said, for perhaps the tenth time.

There was a pause, and she wondered if he expected her to correct herself.

"No, I have not had that joy," he answered finally. – He sounded sad, and she wasn't sure why she had even brought it up. "Do you?"

"Yes, a daughter." – She stood before he could say, "How lovely," or ask about her husband.

Clearly a foolish impulse had prompted her – she wanted nothing less than to talk or think about the past.

"I'm afraid I am simply too tired to go on," – she said, covering a forced yawn. "I'm so sorry Mr. Leveson, but I must retire." She stretched, and he rose too.

"Well then," he said, taking her hand. "I wish you pleasant dreams." And he kissed the backs of her fingers.

She gave an almost inaudible "Oh!" before once more gathering her decades' worth of training in how to appear always cool and collected. "Thank you," she added with what she hoped was a gracious but distant smile and walked slowly away, suddenly conscious of how much her hips must be on display in her riding kit.

She awoke early the next morning to a clattering of pans as breakfast was made, and they rode back (blessedly) towards feather beds and indoor plumbing. As they crested a hill, she looked up and was arrested by the sight before her. Sunshine was spilling through a rift in the gray sky, warming the ridgetops ahead of them, casting their oaks and pines into sharper relief. Below she could see but not hear the crash of waves on San Simeon beach. The coastline stretched jaggedly north and south and, far out to sea, another sliver of silvery blue light was breaking through clouds.

Ada inhaled deeply, tasting the salty sweetness of dried grass, marine fog and pine sap. Smells of horse sweat and human sweat intruding after a moment were less poetic, like the knots in her back from sleeping on the ground.

She urged her mare on, spurred onwards herself by the prospect of a bath and perhaps a nap.

Lying on her back, floating with eyes closed, Ada heard only a gentle slosh and echo of water from around the walls and ceiling of the Roman Pool. Others admired its opulence; she loved the cobalt blues of its mosaics. They calmed her almost as much as rocking along to the rhythm of water.

The sensation recalled to her a rocking-chair her mother had given her as a wedding gift. Ada remembered sitting in it in the months when she couldn't seem to conceive, thinking what a strange gift it was, since it was really for their progeny and not for her. Later, she'd sat there rocking Jean on nights when her child wouldn't settle under Nanny's care or on nights when she, Ada, wanted to avoid overtures from Harry. Her body was still healing from birth, she had told herself, even as she knew she would never welcome his touch again.

She would sit there rocking, crying over her sleeping child as she planned her escape, knowing that her only chance for happiness was to make a full break with Harry, and that little Jean would be better off staying with her parents in Alta Dena than wherever a scarlet-letter mother might take her. Of course, in the end, people had been more forgiving of her divorce than one might have anticipated. People often were, when money and power were involved. Somehow Ada had persuaded her father (over Mother's protests) to let her have a position on the board of one of his women's interest magazines. In time, an invitation to Hearst Castle had been extended – thanks to her new 'fast' social circle mainly, rather than business sense. Still, she'd put her turn of sitting next to Mr. Hearst to good use as a budding journalist...

Now she sat in the sand some distance away from the elaborate picnic laid out for their party. She knew she would not be missed for a bit and wanted time to stare at the ocean, searching for spumes of white that meant whales, or even – what had never lost its thrill for her – to see them breaching. Theirs was the only group of merrymakers at the cove, and when Ada looked to her left she could imagine she was alone.

She was musing, in fact, on that great day of liberation when she had driven herself to La Jolla and walked alone into the sea, deciding to leave Harry forever, when a voice said:

"Am I disturbing you?"

Solomon's voice always disturbed her, though not in the way he meant. She felt the hair on her arms rise and a ripple of anticipation flow through her.

"No, of course not," she answered, turning to him with a smile which she tried to keep small.

He sat beside her. A white linen suit and Panama hat set off his Mediterranean complexion, and for once there was sun here at the beach, so his wardrobe choice did not seem out of place. On most days of their stay fog had lingered just over the shoreline while it was sunny, hot even, up at the castle.

"I fear I have offended you somehow."

"Oh no!" – Ada adjusted her hat, to avoid looking at him.

He said nothing, waiting.

She considered sitting in silence until he gave up and wandered off, possibly insulted. But she decided the image of his retreating back would be more painful than the prospect of exposing her history to him. – She wasn't sure if that realization thrilled or terrified her.

How to begin? That was usually the hardest part – finding the courage to speak... She cleared her throat once, twice. A third time would certainly elicit an offer to get her a glass of water or wine, but she feared if he left all her mustered resolve would dissipate, so she plunged in *in media res*.

"I'm divorced, you know. My daughter lives with her grandparents when she isn't away at school. Better for her socially, I think." – Ada wondered if he would think her heartless because she divulged all this with dry eyes.

For a time, there was no sound but the mourning cries of gulls and rolling of pebbles as waves sucked in and out down the beach, or an occasional laugh or chink of glassware that drifted over from the rest of the picnickers. Ada didn't want to be the one to break the silence.

"I hear the sadness in your voice," he said at length. "This was a choice you wrestled with."

"Yes." She swallowed. "Not leaving Harry – that was an easy choice really, though the ramifications gave me pause. But letting my parents raise my daughter for the sake of her social standing... I'm still not sure it was the right decision."

She bit her lip. This was far more than she'd intended to say, but Solomon seemed to summon it up from her depths, with his warm dark eyes and his patient quiet.

"I see," he said; and she really did feel that he saw: saw *her*, still young but disenchanted, driving away from the safe, conventional life that had been chosen for her, but trying to preserve that choice for Jean, because maybe Jean would find love where she had found only a cage. "I suppose one confidence deserves another," he continued.

He'd been sitting beside her, so close that he could have reached out and put his hand on her shoulder, though he did not. Now he rose and began wearing a furrow in the sand in front of her, and she felt herself grow anxious in sympathy – or perhaps she just feared what he might reveal.

"I will try your method. Without preamble... I have been married for ten years, but my wife and I have been estranged for the past eight. She claims a divorce is impossible because she is Catholic, but I fail to see the material difference from our current arrangement."

Ada felt her world spin upside down, then right itself with dizzying speed. Giddiness seemed a sole explanation for what prompted her to laugh and say, "Well, we certainly ought to give up this acquaintance immediately. No good can come of two people such as ourselves fraternizing!"

"You are most certainly right." – He beamed back at her, and she felt a different kind of dizziness enveloping her, warm and bubbling and... It made no logical sense, but she was happy! She was reminded unexpectedly of Eve, and for the first time the memory was not purely painful, but bittersweet. Eve would have liked Solomon – urged Ada to take the plunge and damn the consequences. Ada did not know what would come next, but the world seemed full of possibilities previously inaccessible to her.

The others in their party hurried into the very Victorian hotel selected as the coda to their day of exploring down the coast: they were hungry and enticed by its famed Italian cuisine. Truth be told, despite the punctilio of their host, the mood among them was that of schoolchildren on a summer holiday, out from under the prying eyes of their minders. The warm lights from inside the restaurant mingled with a faint evening chill to render the prospect of good food and wine (not rationed, as at the castle) unusually compelling. Yet, as their companions' boisterous conversation faded, neither Ada nor Solomon moved to follow them in.

She felt as if her eyes were linked to his, and found herself moving closer to him. Not trusting herself to look at him for more than a glimpse at a time, Ada turned to take in the view. Standing side by side on the large veranda of the inn, they stared out over the bay to where a full moon hung in the twilit sky and reflected light shuddered on the surface of the water. To distract herself from his nearness, Ada swept her gaze across the entire scene before them, from the train line on their left, to the breakwater on their right, over the boats bobbing at anchor by ramshackle Harford Pier. Despite such dereliction as the Depression had cast over this area, there was a certain magic remaining – magic of a kind that could not be touched by stock market crashes. A seal barked in the distance; a foghorn wailed in response. Ada shivered delightedly, then realized that Solomon was regarding her with great attention.

"I suppose we should join the others," she murmured.

"I suppose we should," he echoed, not moving.

She meant to turn to go – she really did – but she turned into him instead.

He was even closer than before, and she could feel his warm exhalation of surprise on her neck, bringing goose-flesh up on her bare forearms.

"You were just going in, I think," he said, each word sending a vibration along her spine.

Neither of them moved. She felt dizzy again. Glancing away from his stare, she saw a long, slow V of pelicans swooping low over the dusky blue water, their wings silhouetted against the dusky peach sky.

A door to the hotel restaurant creaked, and Ada spun away from Solomon instinctively. Maisie poked her head out: "We have a table, and appetizers and drinks are on the way. I'd get in here soon if you want more than a soup bone!"

Maisie seemed either not to notice or not to care that it was only Ada and Solomon on the veranda, and at close quarters, despite Ada's timely jump. Message delivered, she turned unceremoniously and disappeared back inside.

Ada sighed deeply as she started to follow her friend. She couldn't help regretting something she didn't quite dare name, even to herself. But then, his hand closed firmly over her upper arm and drew her irrevocably back toward him; and she allowed herself to be drawn.

*

A sense of the impermanence of life had never been clearer to her than on that day, holding to him in that moment as if she could freeze herself in it, never having to break out of their embrace or say goodbye a last time, to know one another's touch and timbre of voice and scent only forever in memory. Ada choked on a sob. She would have given the very skin off her body, or ribs from her side, to be with him until they grew gray and one of them died. But the one thing she could never sacrifice – further than she had already done – was her daughter's life, and a divorcée running off with a married man was nothing if not a recipe for scandal.

They were lucky, she thought, that she hadn't become pregnant. A tear snaked down her cheek as she remembered – if only! Then she would have *had* to choose to stay with him as the lesser scandal to being a pregnant divorcée. Why did these things never happen when you most hoped (and feared) that they would?

She smelled his sweet, spicy scent on her arms long after their last embrace. It was exquisite torture to catch a whiff of it in memory as she went about succeeding days like a sleep-walker. Her heart sometimes yearned towards him with such intensity that she half-expected it to reach right out of her body in search of him. Conventional wisdom said that time would help her forget, but that was part of the pain of it all – she could not bear the thought of ever forgetting what had been theirs. And it cut her to the core to think that he might come to feel differently about her.

She felt again a sudden, intense stab of the loss of Eve. She longed to hear what her dead friend might say – comfort, advice, even satirical wit might have been welcome, so long as it came from a beloved source.

II.

Jean

The way was, at long last, shadowed by eucalypti. After driving along a broad avenue, they veered onto a smaller road that began slowly to spiral downward. Jean felt a familiar leap of her heart as she caught a first glimpse of the Pacific below, winking blue and brilliant under an afternoon sun. They doubled back as the road snaked around, and she got a fuller glimpse of La Jolla. Waves crashed against the point beyond the Cove, then the land curved shell-like along the sea's edge, from honey-colored cliffs and caves to sandy beaches backed by rust-red Spanish tiled roofs. The adobe buildings and lawns of the Beach Club made a bright patchwork from this distance. Nearer to hand were the buildings and pier of the Scripps Institution of Oceanography, founded by the great and good Ellen Browning Scripps, who had also helped to found Jean's *alma mater*, The Bishop's School.

The gang decided to go straight for refreshment: driving was thirsty work. They pulled into the Club driveway, lined by towering palms, and wound past a raucous duck pond until they at last arrived at a flagstone-floored entryway bordered with snapdragons in flowerpots.

Jean had a sense of homecoming.

It was still too hot to sit in the full sun in comfort, so they drew stools up to the bar and ordered a round of mint juleps. The bartender remembered her, despite Jean being a less frequent visitor at the Club since matriculating at Stanford. The bourbon put them in an even giddier mood than the one in which they'd arrived, and they decided a quick dip in the sea would restore them further from the sweltering journey.

An attendant helped them take their essentials to the women's locker rooms, and in short order they were at the water's edge, laughing and dipping their toes into pleasantly cooling wavelets. Jean had a flash of memory: she had stood in this exact spot as a girl, calling to Nana to watch her swim. Nana and Grandfather had brought her to the Club most summers after her parents' divorce. Adults occasionally spoke about The Divorce in whispers, but never to her face, so Jean did not speak of it either. Father was nearly always taken up with his practice, and Mother had traveled a great deal before she met Donald and relocated to Portland. Thus it had fallen to Nana and Grandfather to take Jean on vacation when she was out of school and her parents were otherwise engaged. Often they would bring her cousins along too, which helped soften the lonesome ache, somewhat.

Jean shrugged off the melancholy that crept over her when she thought of her parents' absence. Someday she would have her own family and would do things differently.

One of the Stanford boys whom they'd run across (a friend of a friend) was holding forth at length on how America must solidify her position as leader of 'the free world'. Sarah listened, apparently enthralled. Jean thought he was quite an attractive specimen, but looks only got one so far: sooner or later a dull personality couldn't help but cast a pall over the most chiseled features or physique.

She selected another Lucky and fitted it into her holder, then looked around for a light. Mr. Stanford was still lecturing whoever would listen, which seemed to be all the girls sunbathing with Jean by the pool. She must have left her book of matches somewhere – couldn't find them in her bag – but just as she was contemplating how to stem the torrent of words long enough to ask for a light, her attention was caught from across the pool by a man in military khaki.

He was in a party of three or, rather, four, but the girls and the other man hardly made an impression on Jean. They were just entering the pool area near the tennis leaderboard, and Jean watched as he joked and laughed with the girl beside him. His uniform set off broad shoulders and his height to advantage, but Jean sensed that there was something more keeping her eyes on him.

As his group crossed toward the dining room, he glanced in her direction. Their eyes locked, and Jean's heart began to pound in her throat. Murmuring a word to his companions, he started towards her. Jean didn't consider herself the shrinking damsel type, but for a moment she thought she might faint. Then she endeavored to call to mind what Nana and Mother had drilled into her: shoulders back, chin up... The rest was escaping her, somehow.

"I hate to see anyone suffer for lack of a light," he said, drawing near.

"Oh, thank you," she answered lamely, eyes on his hands as he deftly struck a match and lit her cigarette.

"I'm Andrew. Lieutenant Andrew Grey, if we're being formal."

"Jean – Jean Campbell." She extended her free hand, and he took it.

What next? All her Stanford dates hadn't prepared her for this dizzy spiraling between her head and her chest.

Fortunately, Lieutenant Grey did not seem in the least perturbed by her awkwardness.

"My friends and I are here for lunch. Care to join us for a drink afterward?" – His look seemed to exclude the Stanford lecturer and *coterie*, which suited Jean just fine.

Who was this Princeton man anyway? Why did he get under her skin so, with his stubborn jaw and the uncompromising angles of his face? She found herself unaccountably frustrated when she and the crew went out and he wasn't there, even though there were hordes of other good dancers to hand.

One night, for example, they were at the Casa, and plenty of nice-looking men were asking her to dance, yet Jean had the disquieting feeling that the night would not begin until she saw Andrew – *if* she saw him. It was appalling to be *so* absorbed in the presence (or absence) of one man that she kept getting caught out in conversations, not knowing what she was expected to say next. Fortunately, it was usually expedient to murmur "Mhmm" in soothing tones and lean her head against her partners' chests. They seemed not to notice she hadn't answered their questions.

The band struck up one of her favorites, Duke Ellington's "Prelude to a Kiss", and Jean fumbled in her clutch to avoid the eye of a youth who displayed an alarming number of teeth when he smiled and had evinced no sense of rhythm when they'd danced earlier to "Am I Blue?" He finally wandered off in another direction, and Jean exhaled and leaned against the wall, instantly reminding herself of an ungainly phase at Bishop's, when she'd often done time as a wallflower. Fixing her gaze on the revolving couples, Jean determined to find entertainment from them, if not inspiration from the female half's choice of dress. For all its wonderful qualities, La Jolla was not nearly so fashion-forward as San Francisco.

"An unexpected sight. The belle of the ball not dancing?"

She turned with a start. "Oh, it's you." She coughed in an attempt to justify the tremor in her voice.

His laugh was full and free. "Don't be too disappointed. It's the best I can do. If you can overlook that one fatal flaw, though, perhaps I can convince you to dance? This song is a real toe-tapper."

Jean thought about making him work for it a bit, but already he had taken her hand and was leading her onto the floor, and she couldn't even have said whether she'd answered him with words or not.

He placed his hand on the small of her back, and she felt a shiver run down it. He started and looked at her sharply. Had he felt it too, then? Not her shiver, but the current that had surged between them as he drew her close?

*

Jean stretched grumpily. It was barely light. Why had her alarm just gone off? She rolled over and was nearly back to sleep when she remembered: she'd promised to go swimming with Madge at the Cove. Silently she cursed her optimism of the night before, no doubt inspired by a generous number of martinis at the Marine Room. They'd progressed there from La Cita, where Nana had given them an excellent dinner with plenty of vino.

Oh well, no help for it now but to swim it off – hopefully. Jean slipped her knapsack over her shoulders and went out via the garden to get her bike. A spray of bougainvillea brushed her face, leaving tendrils of dew on her cheek. The air was heavy with a voluptuous scent of jasmine.

On early mornings like this it was silly to ask for the car – especially when she was going such a short distance. Mother might not approve, but Mother was in Portland. She had told Jean more than once that men did not like women who were too independent, and Jean sometimes had wondered if that's why Mother and Father had gotten divorced.

She wheeled her bike around to the front and set off down the wide, empty street. Barely a palm frond moved, and only one or two of the neighbors' help hurried along the sidewalk, probably towards the bakery. A few sleek sedans carried all-night revelers home to breakfast and coffee in bed.

As she rounded a corner and a breeze off the ocean caught her, Jean momentarily regretted not having worn her sweater, which was still hanging in the hall at home. But already the sun's rays were starting to warm her back, and something about the smell of sea and grass and evaporating dew told her today would be pleasantly hot for mid-September.

Madge arrived as Jean was parking her bike, and they made their way down to the water together. Jean paused on a large rock to take in the view – the ocean still as a lake, refracting honeyed morning light in shades of blush and silver – then hurried on after Madge.

Standing in shadows cast by the rocks, they changed, pulled on their swim caps and dipped their toes in the water. Looking at each other, they shivered.

"Just think of all the cakes we can eat at supper tonight," Madge said, sounding only half-convinced.

This time of year, the ocean was still quite warm; it was just a problem of getting in. Not giving herself time even to think of summoning courage, Jean waded out. She resisted an impulse to stop when the water met her waist, then her chest. A small wave formed ahead, and she dove into it, then flipped onto her back, spluttering slightly, but finally enjoying the feel of the saltwater against her skin.

It was not difficult to get beyond the spume of light shore-break to where the sea rose and fell gently, like the breathing of a great being. A sea lion poked its head out of the water next to them and swam about 20 yards beside Jean before being distracted by a small school of fish. Jean lost herself in the rhythmic slice of her body through shallow swells. By the time they'd finished swimming, the sun had warmed the sand sufficiently so they could lay out their towels and sun themselves like the seals at the Children's Pool nearby.

*

Everyone except Andrew and Jean was getting loaded tonight. After Beau had leaned across her for the third time to flirt clumsily with Sarah, Jean could feel her good mood evaporating. She sighed into her martini glass. Then Andrew, who stood leaning against the bar, annoyingly too far away to talk to, caught her eye and tilted his head toward the double doors. She hesitated. He repeated the gesture.

She set down her drink and stood, murmuring apologies around their booth as she inched her way out. Andrew turned and exited through the heavy, embossed doors just ahead of her. Before she had time to get really incensed at his rudeness, she found him waiting outside.

"No need to give the gossips any more ammunition," he said as he fell in beside her, hands in pockets.

He grinned, and as though by common consent they strolled out to the esplanade. A westering sun hovered low over the horizon, painting nearby clouds a molten gold and tinging the further sky with lilac.

They came to steps leading down to the beach, and Andrew quirked an eyebrow at her. She kicked off her pumps and set them with her handbag on the breakwater. He removed his loafers and socks and rolled up his trousers. Then he offered her his arm.

She wondered, when they reached the water's edge, if he expected her to release him. She did not.

They walked along the shushing ocean, watching gulls carve slow wheels in amber light, pelicans dive into the surf for their dinner and the sun reflect off the cliffs above Scripps Pier. Andrew told her about growing up on a lake in Minnesota, about sailboat races and hockey and mosquitoes as big as rats. He also spoke of his only brother, Malcolm, two years his junior, of whom he clearly thought the world.

Jean talked about drives down to La Jolla from Alta Dena as a child, when the Club was nearly a yacht club instead of a tennis club and her eccentric maiden great-aunts, Ellen and Virginia, still lived in a cottage nearby.

Strange, she thought, how someone she'd known for a matter of a week or two should seem so familiar, so home-like. Although, whenever she caught his eye as he looked down at her, her stomach fluttered with an unfamiliar but pleasant sort of queasiness.

At last the sun set in earnest, palms and buildings near the horizon turned to silhouettes against a sky of flame, and they realized they would be missed by their friends. Reluctantly, they turned their footsteps back toward the bar. Just before they reached the lighted esplanade, Andrew drew her into the deeper shadow of a pillar. Her heart beat so hard that she was sure he could hear it. She reminded herself that she'd kissed plenty of boys before, but it did not seem to matter.

Eventually, they went in to the bar to find the others gone. The gang had left word that she and Andrew should join them in the Marine Room for dinner and dancing.

"Sounds like a good time," he smiled.

Joining hands, they walked out past the moonlit pool and along the esplanade in the opposite direction.

They swung their clasped hands like kids till they reached the back entrance to the Marine Room. A pianist was playing The Ink Spots' "Into Each Life Some Rain Must Fall." A buzz of conversation, punctuated by laughter and the rattle of a cocktail shaker led them toward the bar, in front of which a few couples were dancing. It was a Tuesday evening, so things were relatively subdued – a circumstance to which their party seemed oblivious. Now, however, Jean found herself completely unperturbed by their antics.

She and Andrew drove uptown, They passed the road that would take them to the Cove, then the Colonial Hotel, then St. James-by-the-Sea and finally Bishop's School. A wave of mingled nostalgia and discomfort swept over Jean as she gazed at its saffron walls and adobe-tiled roofs, its tower and well-trimmed grounds. She wondered how to describe the years of her life spent there in a way Andrew would understand. To communicate the disappointments and hopes, failures and joys of her youthful self required much more than "I was at boarding school there."

It was so powerful, her need to be understood, *known*, by him. She felt she was constantly coming up against limits of language, or at least in her own ability to communicate in language. More than frustrating, it was painful, this inability to bridge the divide between herself and him. The sensation frightened her; it almost made her miss the simplicity of dating men that she found less compelling.

Jean recalled her first date, which had taken place here in uptown La Jolla. She had probably been fourteen or fifteen and could barely force down her dinner, she was so nervous. She had eaten a few bites of roast beef, then pushed the rest around her plate until it looked *almost* like the plates of one of the very slim girls. Jean generally had a hearty appetite and was occasionally admonished by her father (when she saw him for the odd dinner) that she must watch her figure now that she was "becoming a woman".

As soon as permitted, she'd scurried back to her room to slip into a new dress Mother had sent her. It was yellow with bunches of white and blue-gray blossom and highlighted her collarbone in what she felt was a becoming manner. Madge had helped Jean fix her hair and loaned her a large cardigan with which to conceal the not-to-code neckline. Jean had tucked a lipstick into her handbag to apply discreetly in the ladies' room at the movie theater, if she was able to get there before her date. Last of all, she'd put on a gold and pearl necklace that Nana and Grandfather had bought for her in Vietnam. There! As she slipped out of her room, Nancy had come out of the room next door and spritzed her with some contraband Chanel. They'd taken the stairs down together,

Jean trying hard not to run – mustn't be unladylike. Nor must she scuff her patent leather pumps.

Their plan depended on each other. If stopped, she and Nancy would maintain a fiction that no chaperone was needed because they were just two girls going to the movies together. It had taken maneuvering for them to convince their prospective dates independently that they should go on the same Friday evening to see a Fred Astaire musical – neither boy, it transpired, was yet cultured enough to appreciate musicals. They had chosen the night strategically also as one when several teachers would be away and chaperones therefore scarce. In the event, fate had also taken a role. It was the end of the year and some girls and teachers had already left for the summer. Normal rhythms such as evening chapel had ceased early because the chaplain and organist were both ill with a cold that had also laid low many teachers, and of those who remained a few were due for their night off. This insider information had been relayed by Madge, who worked after school in the office of the headmistress. Madge was so gentle and innocent-looking that no one in authority would suspect her of aiding and abetting her fellow-students in flouting the rules. Indeed, it had taken some coaxing to convince Madge that she wasn't abandoning her morals by helping Jean and Nancy to sneak out *with boys*…

Andrew was late. He'd said he'd pick her up at 7pm and it was now 7.45pm. Andrew was never early, but he'd never made her wait before and Jean, who a few minutes earlier had been busy applying lipstick, blissfully ignorant of the time, now watched the clock in Nana's sitting room with crossed arms, tapping one finger of her gloved right hand against her left elbow. She had swept down the stairs fully expecting him to greet her, bourbon in hand and a smile of admiration on his handsome face. Her new gown hit at just the right point on her calves, accentuating her ankles, which she knew he liked. But the room was empty and no one home to tell her if Andrew had even telephoned to explain his tardiness.

She tried reasoning with herself – could he have a flat tire? She had been very late in getting ready anyway... None of it helped. A steady flame of anger took hold, burning all the more hotly because she knew deep down that she was being irrational. She poured herself a whiskey and soda and put a record on at random. It was the King Cole Trio, a favorite of theirs. She rose again to change it, but before she could, someone knocked and then immediately entered. She didn't have time to recross her arms before he was in the room and in front of her in a few long strides.

Only then did he appear to notice the expression on her face. "What's wrong?"

His eyes were concerned, but she steeled her heart, turned away and looked pointedly at the clock.

"Ah yes, sorry I'm a little late."

"A little?!"

"Well, all right then –" His conciliatory tone jangled against her taut nerves.

"It may come as a surprise to you, but if you're not keen, there are plenty of men who'd be happy to take your place!" – She fought back tears at a thought that maybe he was just amusing himself with her while she'd been falling for him. "No need," she continued, as he opened his mouth, "to make me wait around for you while you make up your mind."

She knew she was being impetuous and hotheaded and all things she usually was not, but there was a certain catharsis in venting her pent-up fears along with her anger. She drew herself up. No doubt he'd want to leave now if he hadn't before, but she wouldn't give him the satisfaction of going on his own terms. "Perhaps you'd better leave," she heard herself saying, even as her heart protested "No!"

"I'll leave if you want me to." – Andrew's voice was quiet, his body still.

She summoned her nerve and looked him in the eye at last. He did not look angry. Sad and frustrated, confused perhaps. How could he be so patient with her?

But he was talking: "I think you should know why I was late, Jean. I was receiving my orders. We're shipping out next week." He said it so calmly that it took a beat for the words to sink in. When they did, the thread by which she had been holding herself together came undone and she burst into tears and flung herself at him in the same moment.

Slowly he brought a hand up to the base of her neck and stroked it while murmuring soothing words in her ear.

She gasped out "So sorry" and "Oh Andrew!" repeatedly, but was caught by a fresh wave of weeping whenever she tried to say more.

"It's okay," he said, over and over.

Finally she was calm enough to protest. "No," (sniff) "no, Andrew, I ought to be the one comforting you. And instead, I –" (deep, shaking breath) "I attacked you!"

"I *was* very late." He smiled that cockeyed smile of his.

"But," she could only say it in a whisper, "I was only ready about ten minutes before you arrived."

He was quiet for so long that she drew back, certain he must be glaring down at her. She looked up into his face. He was doing his damnedest not to laugh!

*

It was a silly thing to feel loss over. Yet every year, it felt like a little death when the days turned suddenly so much shorter and she came out of a lecture to lit street-lamps and encroaching night. On weekends the afternoons grew pale earlier and light fled across the foothills to the west.

It was the beginning of the end of the old year. "'We'll go no more a-roving'," Jean thought sadly, then laughed at herself for being so sentimental. After all, in a few months, it would all begin to go the other way again. Still, a little voice whispered, *you'll never have this year back.*

What a year it had been – and still not quite over. This year, she felt sure, she'd met her husband. Yet which one was he? That voice in her head whispered that she already knew, but she ignored it. She wasn't superstitious, but she wouldn't chance jinxing things by being too sure. Besides, one had to do something while waiting for an unnamed man to return from overseas, and it was nice to let the other ones believe that they had a fighting chance. Such polite fictions were easiest if you (almost) believed them too.

One of those other suitors was McDonnell. Jean recalled one occasion in particular when, as was his habit, he'd placed a hand on the small of her back and steered her toward the dance floor. She'd set down her martini as they passed a high table and let herself be drawn. They'd settled into a foxtrot as the band drew its breath after a fast number. Other couples eddied around the dimly lit room, most of the fellows in military dress. Jean knew it wasn't patriotic of her, but all the uniforms gave her a chill. After all, how many of these men, laughing and dancing and drinking champagne, would lie dead on a battlefield far away before the old year was spent?

McDonnell chose that moment to lean in for a kiss – she averted her head for a second before remembering herself. They *were* here on a date, and she liked McDonnell – most of the time. Sometimes he was overbearing, but, on the other hand, he took her to the finest restaurants and sent flowers whenever he'd behaved really badly and they'd had a fight. But then, why did she always feel something was missing? Why did his kisses leave her completely composed?

She sighed as they rotated around the room again. Was she looking for something that only existed in novels or movies? … And in La Jolla, in her memory?

She continued to fret as she awaited a letter from Andrew. She'd always doubted herself, and now most of all when so much of her future happiness seemed to hang on this lone decision. Mother and Nana both urged her not to take too much time deciding – a man like McDonnell would wait only for so long. And though Jean had no shortage of admirers at present, Mother had reminded her last time they'd gone to San Francisco for a day of shopping with Sarah Evans and her mother that Jean would find admirers thinner on the ground as she grew older. Especially now, with a war on, men were ready to commit, but they would grow scarcer as time passed. That was just the sad truth, Mrs. Evans had agreed.

Jean remembered all too well this hope-against-hope waiting for letters, though her mother had never had Andrew's excuse of being in the thick of a war. Generally, she had been on a yacht in the Caribbean or visiting a glamorous set of friends – at Hearst Castle, perhaps – or up in Portland with her unobjectionable second husband, Donald.

Sometimes Jean's own letters to her mother had had to be forwarded more than once; sometimes they'd been returned, envelope smudged and address no longer legible. Usually Mother had written back in reasonable time, though it might have been only a hasty scrawl on a postcard. Then there were the letters with vivid accounts of elaborate house parties: what they ate, who wore what, which cocktails they drank as they watched the sun set from some promontory. More ordinary letters had taken a maternal tone, advising on clothes or asking Jean what she required for her new year of school. There were many letters, but the wait between them had always been painful – especially because, every now and then, a letter of Jean's was never answered and no explanation or apology was ever offered.

But Andrew... though he made fewer promises than any of the other fellows she dated, Jean believed him when he said simply that he would write to her the first chance he got. As the weeks dragged by, her conviction faltered at times, but she would call to mind his face as he'd made the promise, firm and determined like his hands holding hers, and she would rally. Then she would go out for drinks with a new guy at Dinah's to lift her spirits, all the time an image of Andrew suspended in the back of her mind like a medallion.

She'd never known a man so hard to forget – not that she wanted to, really.

It was a lovely warm evening for late October, and Jean opened her window all the way and leaned out, anticipating yet another night out with friends. This one would be to celebrate a new engagement in their circle. As she'd written to Mother in a recent letter, it seemed as though couples couldn't get married fast enough now that the war was being seen for what Andrew had always said it would be: a behemoth of an endeavor that would not soon be over.

She liked that word, *behemoth...*

A few nights later Jean observed Sandy and McDonnell from behind an archway festooned with eucalyptus and hothouse orange blossom. A mingled fragrance of aromatic leaves wafted on the breeze, and the Stanford fall social promised to be a shining success, as usual. The live band was full of *joie de vivre*; the food smelled delectable; the cocktails were plentiful and strong. The one fly in the ointment – well, two, really – would not be considered a problem by most. Jean had, by a series of crucial misunderstandings, ended up with two dates, and neither McDonnell nor Sandy seemed to be taking the situation in the humorous vein in which she'd tried to cast it. If only Andrew were here, he would see the comedy in it. He'd also no doubt find a gentlemanly way to tell the other fellows they weren't wanted. But he's *not* here! Jean reminded herself. Anyway, aren't two dates enough of a problem without bringing a third man into it?

Sandy was making awkward (she assumed) conversation, gesticulating with his champagne flute and wetting his whistle. McDonnell, on the other hand, was staring around morosely with hands in his pockets, largely ignoring the other man. McDonnell did have a good profile for frowning, Jean thought, shaking herself and emerging from her hiding place with fresh drinks in hand. She must get the two of them back inside the gym and dancing. She had plenty of Theta sisters here, and surely one would willingly help her with her quandary. It wasn't as though either of her dates were ugly.

Sandy relieved her of two flutes of champagne, but did not hand either of them to McDonnell. Suppressing a sigh, Jean gave McDonnell her third flute, then smiled as she accepted one of the first two back from Sandy. Amazing that grown men could be so petty! She reminded herself that she had (more or less) brought this on herself, and now there was nothing to do but make the best of it.

The three of them chinked glasses perfunctorily, and Jean took a long sip. The band struck up a new song and she smiled hopefully at them.

"How about it, boys? You wouldn't want to deprive me of a formative college experience!" – Not that any of the multiplicity of dances and socials she'd attended thus far, however fun, had been life-changing; but she allowed herself this small fiction in pursuit of the greater good.

McDonnell adjusted the gauntlet cuffs of his white dinner jacket. "Far from it. I'll take you in there right now, and Mr. Barrett can take pity on one of the wallflowers."

"Hey –" Sandy started.

"There's no need for anyone to get excited," Jean said, frowning at McDonnell, who beamed back at her.

It was his first smile of the evening. He evidently sensed that he was the favorite and pressed his advantage.

"Much like the Allies," Jean said, feeling as though she were lecturing children, "we three have common interests that can be achieved if we're willing to make compromises."

Moving quickly to preempt a skirmish, she took each of her escorts by an arm and steered them back towards the women's gymnasium. They swung open the double doors and, as they passed into the dim interior, a wave of sound washed over them. The band was extemporizing on a popular song, and couples swayed and laughed in a mass on a large, make-shift dance floor. Bartenders shook cocktails like their lives depended on it, while knots of students and servicemen clustered around the long trestle tables that were filled with cakes and other refreshments.

Jean gazed at what in other circumstances might have seemed like ingredients for a perfect evening. She searched a little desperately for some friend who had come stag or with a partner who'd been waylaid by food and drink. At last, just as both of her dates were growing restive again, she saw Madge carrying a fresh platter of rum cake out from the back. Of course! Madge had been too busy planning the event to find a date, and, critically, she was close enough to call to.

"Madge!" – Jean sensed Sandy standing a little straighter by her side as her friend turned towards them. Jean batted down a momentary annoyance at Sandy, simultaneously administering a little lecture to herself: *Yes, he's my date, but I can't have two, and it's better one goes willingly.*

"Jean!" – Madge gazed bemusedly at her friend's two bodyguards. "You seem," she quirked an eyebrow, "busy." Madge set down the cake. She was looking exceptionally pretty tonight, her blonde hair swept back and her gown setting off a fine décolletage.

"This is Sandy, and this is McDonnell." – Jean gave Sandy a gentle squeeze of the arm and he took the hint.

"Care to dance?" he said to her, extending a hand.

Madge looked to Jean, who vigorously nodded a blessing, and away they went.

"That was either some first-class diplomacy or the devil's own luck," McDonnell said, taking Jean in his arms and spinning her too onto the dance floor.

Jean smiled. "If the world were ruled by women, there'd be no need for wars."

"'Ruled by women'! Saints preserve us!"

"It's been done before – Elizabeth the First, Cleopatra. Not entirely peaceful monarchs, I'll admit, but *they* were surrounded by male advisors."

He smiled down at her patronizingly.

Maybe all of history did not support her bold claim, Jean reflected, but she'd like to see it tried again. Women weren't out to prove their own virility, and therefore, they often came up with solutions that men might overlook as beneath them or too tedious.

Jean gazed at her remaining date. He was handsome and well on his way towards glory in the war and then (she had no doubt) a successful legal career. Her family would love him. But sometimes conversations like this left her cold – not merely dispassionate, but with an icy prickle up the spine. The music changed to "Ain't Misbehavin'", and her mind flitted to Andrew. *Let* him *be the one,* she caught herself thinking, even as McDonnell drew her closer.

A battered letter finally arrived, with its edging of blue and red and Andrew's strong handwriting giving the direction. Jean's stomach spun, and she took the stairs two at a time, yet still it felt like an age before she was flopped on her bed and luxuriating in his words.

There was so much he could not say, and she could almost feel the weight of it – of the horror of war – bleeding through the pages. At the same time, he felt so near as he told her how he thought of her day by day, and night by night...

The phone rang and she ran reluctantly back down to the kitchen to answer, none of her housemates being home to take it. "Jean? Is that you? McDonnell here. Thought I'd ring and see if I could convince you to drink martinis with me at Dinah's tonight, if you're not otherwise engaged."

Jean thought regretfully of her cozy evening re-reading and responding to Andrew's letter, all while smoking a Lucky or two and wearing her favorite house slippers. But Nana's admonition rang in her ears: "Don't set too much store by any one man too soon!" So she said yes, she'd love a martini and loped back upstairs to take her hair out of rollers and at least put on some lipstick and pumps.

What to say to someone coming up against the hard edges of life? Facing the reality that soon the one you love will be not an "is" but a "was", a "used to love" instead of "loves"? Jean had yet to experience such agony; moreover, she thought *she* probably believed in an afterlife, while McDonnell said he did not. She wondered if it was it better to say nothing until he brought up his mother's fatal illness (if he did) or to jump into the breach with words of sympathy, if not comfort?

Andrew had written often of the truth about war. It was neither glorious nor romantic nor, even in the best of circumstances, particularly just, whatever Aquinas might have said. Andrew had written about the men he had lost – men whose names Jean had come to know – and she had felt his sadness seeping across the pages, between his spare yet eloquent words. Jean was at a loss as to what to write in response to those letters, and that same feeling of helplessness was with her now, as she looked into McDonnell's eyes, blank with the impossibility of comprehending his new reality.

Morlini's was gay. Perhaps that's what had led McDonnell to suggest they step in for a drink tonight. A jazz band and an enthusiastic group of officers bent on dancing with every woman in the club lent an atmosphere of celebration to an otherwise average weekday evening, and Jean resolved to leave Andrew and his unit out of mind for now, moldering in the humidity of some tropic island. McDonnell *was* very handsome after all. He deserved a fair shot. Before she met Andrew, he'd been the frontrunner by a mile.

One drink turned into several, and she found herself longing for supper – not just the mixed nuts they served with drinks. She stood up to go to the ladies' and felt herself sway in a way highly suggestive of inebriation. Her cheeks burned and she drew a deep breath while her hand still lay on the chrome bar. Then she walked carefully away, acutely conscious of her high, slingback pumps.

Jean took her time, fixing her lipstick and dabbing the shine off her nose, before rejoining McDonnell. She noted with dismay that he had ordered *more* drinks in her absence and was nearly finished with his. He was talking to the bartender at a volume that carried well beyond the circle of friends and acquaintances who'd accumulated around them. As Jean reclaimed her stool, she laid a hand on his arm.

"I'm famished!" she said – only a slight exaggeration. "How about something to eat?"

"I can get you a booth." The bartender waved to a hostess.

"No, no! We're having a fine time here! Let's just get some of those mussels in white wine and some bread to have at the bar. We can go somewhere else later."

Jean prepared to protest, but the bartender put in their order and turned to another patron. She sighed and sipped her martini carefully.

The mussels came, fragrant with garlic and butter, and it was all Jean could do to eat in a somewhat dainty manner. McDonnell hardly touched his portion, but ordered yet another round of martinis. She flatly refused to drink hers. *She knew her limits.* He put his hand on her back from time to time, which might have been meant as reassuring or an affectionate gesture, but each time his hand slipped lower, until he was practically grabbing the stool she was sitting on.

She didn't often get angry, but Jean's blood was beginning to simmer. Here McDonnell was, dragging her out on a cold evening when she ought to be studying for an economics exam, only to get plastered and take liberties with her! She was concocting the perfect scathing thing to say the next time he touched her when their eyes met and she saw desolation in his. His mother! How could she be so quick to forget? Madge had told her that Mrs. McDonnell's breast cancer was not expected to let her last out the week.

There it was – the incontrovertible and highly inconvenient fact that while McDonnell and the others took her to the swankiest clubs, sent dozens of roses, kissed her at just the right moment as the moon floated over San Francisco Bay, it was Andrew who Jean was in love with. How had he said it in that letter she kept under her pillow?

If you've ever watched the sun break through a fog over the ocean, turning slate gray, oily seas into brilliant jade and aquamarine, illuminating the grass and flowers of the bluffs in the foreground, almost as if calling them into being for the first time, then you know what it is to have the veil of familiarity pulled back and to glimpse for a moment the mysterious, abiding glory of existence. If you've known this experience, but instead of the glory of nature, it's the glory of another human face that has gifted you with a fresh way of seeing, then you know what it is to love.

Re-reading this still brought on a mostly pleasant pain at her heart. After this letter, it seemed less a decision than an inevitability that she *would* marry Andrew – that was that. And when he stepped out of a cab one December day, closing the door and adjusting his collar as he looked up at the house with a familiar, but until then forgotten, squint, Jean felt her heart expand in a way that, until that moment, she had never experienced. Any lingering idea of another suitor melted like foam on the surface of the sea.

She dashed downstairs, heedless of Nana's many lectures on decorum, and threw open the door just as he knocked. Sudden shyness at having been apart for so long seemed to capture them both, and they froze. Jean hoped he would wrap her in his arms, even as she noticed how jagged the planes of his face had become and how loosely his officer's uniform now fitted. Finally, she summoned her resolve and met his gaze. How weary he looked around the eyes! But the message in them was only love. A small sob escaped her, and the next thing she knew she was burying her face in his coat as his arms tightly enfolded her.

They stood so for a few minutes, his hand softly stroking her hair, and she realized he was probably very tired and also that she was too nervous to look at him directly again. But she willed herself to do so. And then they were kissing, and all thought of how tired he must be vanished.

In time, they came inside, and Jean made cocktails and brought out the *hors d'oeuvres* she'd prepared carefully from a *Better Homes & Gardens* clipping after his phone call informing her of his arrival. They ate at the kitchen table, holding hands whenever they weren't sipping their drinks.

"I only have two weeks before I have to collect my new orders, and I've told my family I'd visit home for one."

"After they pushed you to the limits of human endurance for the past two *years*?"

"Uncle Sam is short on gratitude in times of war."

Jean sniffed, somewhere between outrage and tears. Here she'd been planning weeks of drinks and dinner after work (her cooking now and then, plus lots of good restaurants) and outings to the beach or to art galleries on weekends! In her imaginings, only by the end of *many months* would he be preparing to visit his family prior to shipping out, and he would suddenly find himself unable to bear the idea of their being parted again unless he were sure of her. They would be standing on the Golden Gate Bridge looking out to the sea beyond the headlands of Marin, and he would turn to her and ask for her hand and then suggest taking her with him back to that lake in Minnesota to meet his family... Jean of course knew it was unlikely that all would go according to her script, but she had hoped they would have enough time together that she could reasonably expect a ring by the end of it. Now, however, with only a week to spare...

"Well, what do you say?" – From the way Andrew was looking at her, she had the feeling that he had just said something important.

"I – ah," she hesitated, but gave up on the idea of improvising an answer without knowing the question. "Could you say that again?"

"How about if you take the week off work and we spend every last second of it together?"

*

Jean watched the cypress trees, ever more pressed and sculpted by the wind, and felt rightness settle within her. She took a deep inhalation of salt-sweet air: the perfume of mingled sea and seaweed, buckwheat and sagebrush and sun-warmed earth. She had spent so many nights agonizing over the question of whom she should marry, and now that it was officially decided she couldn't believe there had ever been any doubt. It was as if there were an Andrew-shaped lock on her heart, which of course only he could open.

She stood at the top of the sweeping staircase at The Laurels, trying not to freeze up at the knees. Every time she shifted her weight from one foot to the other, the heavy satin of her dress rustled like the breeze blowing through the pines above Half Moon Bay that day Andrew had proposed to her.

The string quartet began to play, and she forced herself to breathe. There was no reason to be afraid. She knew whom she was marrying – knew that, in essence, she had wanted this ever since the first moment he'd strode into her field of vision across the Beach Club pool over two years before. Still, her stomach was behaving like an aerial acrobat.

She heard a heavy tread behind her, and Grandfather was taking her arm. Father's refusal to attend had resolved any doubt about who should give her away. (What an odd phrase – as though anyone had the right to 'give' her to another human being, who would... what then? own her?) She smoothed the moon-colored silk of her gown with her free hand and checked that her bouquet was the right way round. The Wedding March from *Lohengrin* blossomed on the air, and they began their slow descent. Jean hadn't even noticed her bridesmaids processing, but there they were at the head of the aisle of chairs along with the priest, the groomsmen and *him*. She felt her heart surge as though it intended to escape out of her chest. To calm herself she tried looking at their guests: Sandy and Madge, who were beaming, no doubt anticipating their own impending nuptials; Grandmother, who had nearly had her way and seen them married in a grand society wedding at the big Episcopal church, reception to follow at The Langham; Mother and her second-husband Donald, whom Jean seemed to know no better now than when she'd met him seven or eight years before.

This was it. The moment little (and big) girls dreamed of and were groomed for, whether they dreamed of it or not. Jean suspected it was nerves that kept sending her mind on tangents when she ought to be focusing on not tripping or, better yet, simply enjoying the moment. She mentally swept aside all other considerations and looked and looked at the man standing before her. His beloved curls, never fully submitting to pomade when, as now, his hair wasn't cropped close per military regulations; his hazel eyes, so light they sometimes looked golden; his hands, which held such reassurance in their strength...

Now Grandfather was placing her hand in Andrew's, and they were turning together to face the priest. The weight of the words they were about to say to each other hit her with their full power. "Forever" is a long time. And what might "for worse" entail? Yet Jean was unafraid. They would be friends and lovers and all that lay in between – perhaps even occasionally enemies or strangers. But they would work at it together, till death, and that was all that mattered.

*

Taking the children to visit their cousins had been her idea. More accurately, it was Jean's cousin they were to visit and the children's second cousins. Andrew was willing, if dubious – he said he wasn't even sure he'd heard of San Luis Obispo – and gamely loaded the car in a thick, early morning fog ("For a week or a month?" he said, eyeing Jean's suitcase). She fixed tuna sandwiches and packed table grapes and the ginger-snaps Eva had baked the day before ("For the kids," though this had been her own favorite lunch since childhood). Bundling Beatrice, Will and little Tom into the station wagon, they began the long drive north from La Jolla.

At Santa Barbara, they stopped and ate on the beach, and the boys ran circles around the picnic blanket until they were tired. With some protest, they all tucked themselves back into the car, where their "stuff" seemed to have grown since they'd left it, and the journey continued. By the time they finally turned onto a rutted white dirt road flanked on one side by large, rambling trees and bumped along it for a mile or two, everyone's anticipation had begun to turn into impatience. At last, after following the road up a long, curving hill, they were greeted by a pair of barking, tail-wagging dogs and a flurry of chickens and children. Jean's cousin Liz emerged from a gracious single-story house in an apron. Her husband Bill was, presumably, out working somewhere on the property.

Watching the children enjoy themselves was one of the great joys of Jean's life now. Perhaps because she herself had been an only child, it gladdened her to see Beatrice making up a story that they all played along to, or Will taking care of his little brother when Tom scraped a knee trying to scramble up a tree after his older sister. There was a tang of bitter-sweetness as Jean watched, recalling the many days she'd spent playing alone with dolls at Nana's and Grandfather's, hoping her cousins might not come again to visit soon. True, there hadn't been many quarrels, but the ones she'd had with the occasional young visitors had been more devastating to her since she'd had so little practice.

Liz joined her on the porch with two mugs of coffee. All seven cousins were currently intent on reenacting a version of Robin Hood and his Merry Men, instigated by Beatrice.

"Where do they get it?"

"Get what?" Jean asked, taking a steaming sip.

"All that energy. At eight o'clock in the morning!" – Liz looked out at the dusty yard, laughing.

Later that day, they gathered the children together and caravanned up to Big Sur for a few nights of camping along cliffs overlooking the jagged coast.

Rocks poked out of the blue-gray-green sea like the teeth of some impossibly large beast. Windblown cypresses shaded their firepit as they sat around the smoky flames, roasting hot dogs. When everyone had eaten their fill and washing up was done, they banked the fire and led the children to a grassy area more open to the sky for stargazing.

Jean settled between Beatrice and Tom, Will and Andrew beyond them, and gazed at the night sky while Andrew's voice softly charted the most recognizable constellations. Jean had rarely, if ever, felt so grimy – and they hadn't even spent one night yet! Camping had not been among the talents Nana had thought a young lady should master, and since their marriage Andrew had left Jean to plan the family vacations which, till now, had generally involved staying in modest but well-appointed hotels, cottages or cabins. It had been Liz who'd suggested they drive up to Big Sur for a weekend, getting the neighbor boy to feed the animals who couldn't fend for themselves while they were away.

So here they were, laying on blankets on the ground, dust and smoke in their hair and everywhere else, gazing up at the stars. Jean didn't consider herself a philosophical soul, but it struck her as quite the analogy for life.

"Daddy," Will asked, "what's the North Star for?"

Andrew had been explaining how to locate it from the Big Dipper. Jean could hear the smile in his voice as he answered:

"Well, I don't know what it's *for* exactly, but I know how we humans use it – to navigate; to way-find. It's above our North Pole, so it can help you get home if you're ever lost. It's helped sailors chart their courses for hundreds – maybe thousands – of years."

"Daddy," Tom was not to be outdone by his older brother, "where's the Big Dipper? I don't see it."

As Andrew again tried to describe its outline to their five-year-old, Jean's heart warmed. She wouldn't want to be anywhere else, no matter how gritty she now felt. Listening to her husband detail the shapes of the Big and Little Dippers, the Great and Little Bears, she pondered the mysterious pull of the heavens and how humans, from time immemorial, had gazed up and discovered another world gazing back down at them. However unscientific a thought it was, these constellations seemed not simply super-imposed by human imagination, but actually etched into the cosmos, waiting to be found by those who bothered to look.

The next morning was misty and pleasantly chilly, and the adults stretched their sore backs and drank coffee and stood close around the fire while the kids sleep on, as blissfully, it seemed, as though on featherbeds.

Jean and Liz fried eggs and bacon and camp-toast for breakfast. The children emerged, lured by their noses, and everyone ate like they'd already hiked for half a day. Consulting a guidebook Liz had brought along, they then mapped out a trek, making contingency plans for the youngsters, should one or two of them get too tired.

The second night everyone was more subdued, though hungrier than ever. After supper, they sat watching pelicans and gulls glide over the water against the western sky. At last the sun set, leaving a diffuse glory which gathered to a center around a trail of pink cloud that looked like the ethereal skeleton of Leviathan. (Biblical imagery seemed so apt where sea and sky and wilderness met!) Shades of peach and aqua left the pines in black relief, lonely guardians against darkness. In time, the creature in the sky turned magenta with ever-growing streaks of lavender and indigo. Only with difficulty did Jean tear herself away from the view as Tom and Will began to beg for marshmallows.

They stopped at Thrifty's for ice cream on their way back to Liz's and Bill's, then walked along a creekside path up to Mission San Luis Obispo de Tolosa. Its whitewashed façade reflected sun back into their faces as they approached. They poked their heads through the ponderous wood-and-iron doors and found the sanctuary empty. Before the adults could decide whether to enter, Jean's youngest niece, Patty, took off running up the central aisle. The other kids whooped and followed, and Jean found herself shushing and running after them with Liz, both women trying to move respectfully but rapidly through the cavernous nave.

They didn't catch up to their seven sweaty offspring until the children reached the altar. Just then, out of the side nave, emerged a priest.

Jean froze in the act of grabbing Will by the back of his shirt collar. She always found herself noticing details at the wrong moment. Things she normally only sensed in her subconscious forced their way up during moments of stress, and now she was aware of a spicy, musty tang of incense mingling with exhalations of the old building and a shaft of sunlight from an open side door painting a swath of bright peach onto the tiles of the floor. There was a sound of feet shuffling as the children dropped back behind their mothers. Jean cast a panicky glance back down the aisle; it was bordered by swirling vines and flowers that seemed incongruous with the prominent crucifix and gilt saints' icons near the altar. She spotted Andrew and Bill sitting in a back pew looking as though they could be chuckling, though it was hard to tell so far away, and she felt her face and neck tingle with blood – a mix of irritation and embarrassment, with a dash of humor at the spectacle their group made.

Liz spoke first. "We're so sorry, Father." – She crossed herself rustily.

A firm line of mouth under a heavy thicket of moustache broke into a wide smile. "Not at all! Our Lord told his disciples to let the little children come to him, and far be it from me to forbid them!"

*

Andrew looked across the living room and smiled as their eyes caught and held. She loved that about him. He could be in the midst of a conversation with an international business-man, a potential client or a beautiful woman who (as now) was clearly coming onto him, yet he always went out of his way to ensure that Jean knew he was thinking of *her*.

They had mastered the art of carrying on a sort of silent commentary on their individual conversations with a tilt of the head, a twitch of the lips or an eloquent eyebrow. It was one of their favorite pastimes in social situations.

Jean smiled back at him as the beautiful woman moved on in search of easier game. Jean herself was surveying the trays of appetizers circulating, as well as the mood of their guests, making a mental note to have more food brought out in half an hour while giving the appearance of listening to the neighbor at her elbow.

They always had to invite Sam and Charlene or there would be complaints about the noise of the Greys' parties, but two such dull people you'd be hard put to find. Sam was currently describing in agonizing detail the best method for waxing an Aston Martin, and Jean took a long gulp of her cocktail and looked mournfully back at her husband.

The party buzzed along. Soon they were making their signature Green Mumms cocktails with ice cream, crème de menthe and a dash of champagne. People were always ready to dance after a couple of these, and Jean enjoyed watching everyone have a good time. Her satisfaction was greater given that she had a material part in creating that happiness.

"Care to dance?" – Roger's bird-of-prey eyes always made her uneasy, but it was poor form to refuse a dance from one of your guests, so Jean let him guide her out to where other couples were swaying to Elvis Presley's "It's Now or Never." Roger kept his eyes on her as he navigated expertly around the floor; Jean was conscious of his hand on her back, pressing her closer to him than she wanted to be. She smiled tightly, glancing about for Andrew to send a distress signal. But the song came to a close, and Roger dipped her low and held her there until the next song began.

"*Roger!*" she said sharply, as he tried to steer her into the new rhythm; she wanted to knee him between the legs and run, but those were not considered the actions of a lady.

Strange how one minute it was pleasant to have another man's attention, just to be reminded that you were still noticed. Then, as quickly, the other man took your lack of protest as an indication you wished for far more. How could men be so silly? They'd *seen* Andrew, hadn't they? The mere idea that anyone could lure her away was laughable.

Extricating herself from Roger with a murmur about the ladies' room, Jean retreated to the kitchen for a minute before returning to the bar for a drink. She would tell Andrew later and they would never have Roger (and his poor wife) again, but no need to make a scene now. How she hated scenes! They reminded her of being a very young girl lying in her bed in the nursery at the Laurels and hearing raised voices, then tears, on more than one of the rare occasions when her mother had come to visit her at the family home.

Jean roused herself. Fresh air – that's what she needed. Outside votive candles flickered on the high tables by which people mingled. A scent of cigarette smoke, melting wax and blossoming flowers carried on the night breeze. It was a balmy evening, and it felt good to step into the cool.

Jean lit a long-filtered cigarette and leaned against a wall, watching her guests. There really were very few unattractive people here. Actually, there were very few unattractive people in La Jolla altogether. These days, if you didn't like a thing about yourself, there was a doctor who could change it for the asking. Just recently she had run into Sofia, a friend from Texas who came to the Club for a couple weeks every summer. Whereas before Sofia had had quite a small-to-average bust, suddenly her breasts were nearly bursting out of her bathing suit whenever she appeared poolside.

As it transpired, Sofia was here also tonight, standing not twenty feet away from where Jean was leaning. Strange how a change to one's body could affect one's personality so. Before, the Sofia Jean had known had been fun-loving but a little shy; now as she lounged at the center of a group of five or six men, she was obviously and audaciously flirting. Jean observed in astonishment as Sofia sloshed champagne with meticulous aim down the front of the best-looking man there, then ran a slow hand along the stain, one manicured red fingernail lingering near his belt buckle. Jean turned away with the woman's laughter in her ears. She recalled a snatch of conversation overheard a day or two before near the pool between Sofia and another woman of the Texas set. The other woman said something like, "Lucky you. I wish my husband would buy me some new breasts for my birthday!" Sofia had replied, "I wish my husband hadn't thought I needed them."

III.

Beatrice

The lighthouse thundered in Beatrice's memory the way the Pacific beat against the point and the Piedras Blancas, those whiteish rocks that, taken together, looked like a sphinx rising from the sea. The lighthouse itself mesmerized her, with its winding stair and eternally winking light. Its aloneness struck her too, an answering aloneness to the one buried deep inside her. She hadn't realized before that someone could be solitary without being lonely, and that solitude called to her.

She imagined herself the lone lighthouse-keeper. The plaques said something about lighthouse-keepers *and* their families, but she ignored this detail because it was more poetic the other way. Such chosen loneliness meant you weren't really alone: you had the wind, the sea, the elephant seals, gulls, pelicans, rabbits, buckwheat, poppies – a whole world of companionship at your door. And of course she would have a dog, the fourteen-year-old Beatrice had thought: a big, shaggy dog to curl up at her feet on the hearth on a winter's night as she read and a fire cackled and the winds sang sad, cold songs of the sea. From time to time, her family would come to visit her, she had reassured herself, when the image in her mind got a little too eerie.

That visit to the Piedras Blancas Lighthouse was the first thing that had drawn her imagination towards a life of solitude. Funny it had not been one of their visits to Europe, pacing the grounds of some ancient monastery or an abbey full of sand-colored stone and dappled light. The draw had been reinforced every time she had seen another solitary lighthouse standing sentinel along some rugged stretch of their beloved California coast. The religious element to this longing had come more gradually, as she'd studied world religions in college and developed an understanding of her own faith outside of the classroom. The idea of a life consecrated appealed to her, with the relative solitude of a convent holding some of the appeal she'd envisioned in a lighthouse-keeper's vocation to keep the lamp burning.

The red velvet curtain fell, lingering strains of Tchaikovsky died away and audience members moved about gingerly, as though testing whether they were truly in control of their own limbs, after having been bewitched so entirely by *Swan Lake*. Beatrice dashed tears from her eyes as the house lights came up. What must it be like to weave such magic through movement? There had been a time when she thought she might be a ballerina...

Her first ballet slippers had been soft pink leather with matching pink elastic straps across the top. Only girls who'd been studying ballet for some time were allowed to wear the ones with long ribbons that wound up their legs and square toe-boxes on which they could practice their pointe work. Beatrice recalled an unutterable thrill in her six-year-old heart as she'd tried on a peach-colored leotard with a diagonal ruffle across the front. Joy of joys, she got to select a frothy rose tutu and a pair of white tights to complete the ensemble.

For her first performance, her hair had been in two little buns, one above each ear, and she got to hold a wand adorned with pink and blue ribbons and glittering streamers. The dance itself was chaos; she couldn't remember her steps, and neither could most of the other girls in the beginners' class performance. But she only knew this in retrospect. At the time it was the most thrilling experience, with footlights, classical music and a cheering audience.

It took years before Beatrice began to be scared of what people watching her might think. Times came of battling performance jitters; her symptoms ran the gamut from stomachaches to knocking knees to sweating palms. Other moments, however, made it all worthwhile: those moments in performances where she was able to lose herself in the story the music and dancers were telling, her body becoming only one refrain in the larger narrative. Eventually Beatrice realized that it was the music, not the dancing, that spoke to her most – that captured her soul and imagination. For a brief period she'd tried to study both ballet and piano, but her grades had suffered, and in the end, music won.

The first time Beatrice had been moved to tears by music was a memory she cherished in the way some girls cherished the memory of a first kiss (hers had not been memorable). She didn't count the time Mother had taken her to see *Swan Lake* when she was eight: it had been difficult to disentangle the musical storytelling from the dancing, and she suspected that she wept more for the fate of the prince and swan princess than for the expressiveness of the strings. At age twelve, though, hearing Smetana's "The Moldau" for the first time, the music had reached down into her and pulled her inside out. It was a pleasure that had slid seamlessly into pain and back out again.

Years later, as an exchange student, one of Beatrice's favorite remedies when she was in need of a fresh injection of beauty was Evensong or – better yet – Compline. She would snug herself into an angular pew near the choir stalls in Clare College Chapel, the only light given by candles flickering in front of the choristers and readers' lecterns and by the grand tapers on the altar. A hush was on the air: you were meant to attend Compline in silence (apart from set responses in the service), traditionally right before going to bed.

"The Lord Almighty grant us a quiet night and a perfect end." The words of this service held a peculiar loveliness, but even so they did not transport you in the way the choristers did when they sang *a cappella*. Apparently, it was quite a new thing for women to attend Clare as undergraduates, but Beatrice could hardly imagine the choral music without them. The choir would begin to sing in antiphon, the basses, then altos, tenors and sopranos. Slowly their voices would entwine and their music well in polyphony, crescendoing to an almost unbearable climax, before descending to a soft conclusion; and Beatrice's eyes would brim with tears.

The first crisp bite of an apple would always taste like fall to her. Autumn. The word had a mellifluous sound. It was not especially original to love autumn: poets had written odes to the season, for heaven's sake! Still, that did not lessen its delights. Ever since childhood, when Jack-o-lanterns had both alarmed and charmed her, and Thanksgiving had felt like the culmination of all things good, Beatrice had adored fall.

Even in La Jolla, where you would be hard-pressed to find a deciduous tree turning to flame, she'd felt an affinity for the season. In college, the leaves on the grapevines had turned color along the back roads of Edna Valley, usually just as she was getting ready to drive home for Thanksgiving. Then she'd moved to Cambridge for a year abroad and discovered the unparalleled pleasure of Saturday walks to Grantchester in the resplendent light of October afternoons, the air fresh (cool enough to keep your scarf on) and the Cam winding dreamily through the landscape. A foot-path took you under heavy tree cover at first, then past a cattle guard and onto the Meadows where the path hugged a hedgerow peppered with crimson hawthorn berries. Beyond the hedge, fields of close-cropped golden stubble stood where a harvester had passed, and blackbirds and crows alighted here and there to feed. If you paid attention, you might spot a golden pheasant in a fine coat of copper and emerald stalking through the tall grasses that were still waving in the corners of the fields.

She would follow the path, barely resisting an urge to quote Keats aloud, sometimes encountering a herd of cows before at last coming to the village. If you walked right on to the end of the path, you'd pass the back garden of The Green Man, as well as the gardens of several private residences, before emerging onto the road across from an ancient, lovely parish church. Following the road as it curved left, you came to The Orchard, once a refuge of poets and philosophers, now a teahouse among mature apple trees. If it was fine weather and not too late, nothing could compare to the joy of tea and a scone with jam and cream under the late-ripening fruit. Then, a companionable ramble among the yellow-leaved trees and weathering tombstones of the Church of St. Andrew and St. Mary while the light still lingered, thence to the pub...

In summer, Beatrice might meet her Philosophy of Religion friend (well, there were many, but only Anna Mackay did she think of as *the* friend) for fish and chips and beer at The Green Man. They would sit in the back garden for hours discussing life's mysteries, while the locals puffed pipes and consumed an impressive amount of good English bitter without so much as slurring a word. As evenings drew in though, Beatrice liked best to find a snug nook in view of the fire at The Blue Ball Inn, a pub a bit more removed from the rest of the village.

A local band played there most Friday nights, of variable quality but unquestionable enthusiasm. What was of invariably high quality was the food. If a mist rose off the river and the night was chill, few things felt as right as a steak and ale pie and a pint. If she were alone, Beatrice would sit at a corner table and watch the goings on about her from behind a flickering candle: the jovial barkeep and his wife, pulling pints and joking with regulars; the more heavily lubricated patrons singing or dancing along with the band; a placid dog or two asleep on the floor beneath their masters' tables.

If Beatrice came with friends, the night would fly by with a combination of witty banter, intense theological discussion and obscure literary references.

One particularly fine autumn evening, Beatrice sat tucked in a corner of The Blue Ball Inn with Anna, newly minted a doctor of Religious Philosophy. A good number of theological questions had been bubbling up as Beatrice read and wrote and reflected, and she had finally imbibed enough alcohol to summon the courage to pose her questions to Anna.

Leaning over her pint, voice a little shaky, Beatrice whispered, "How can life be so wonderful and yet so terrible? So beautiful one moment and so tragic the next?" She paused, then determined to ask it all: "And, though I'm ashamed to admit it, what bothers me almost as much: how can life be just plain uninspiring so much of the time?"

"Ah yes, the true enemy of all those with the soul of a Romantic: the *quotidien*-ness of sweeping floors or changing nappies!" – Anna's Scottish roll of the 'r' in *Romantic* made it sound even more so than when Beatrice used the word.

"I know those things have their place," Beatrice hastened to add. "And maybe even, looked at from another angle, a strange kind of beauty. But I still hate chores." – She laughed, then frowned. "There *are* things in this world though that are undeniably ugly, and no amount of Pollyanna aphorisms can make a terrible thing good."

Anna put a hand on her arm, and Beatrice realized she had tears welling. "Yes, our capacity to harm is as terrifying as our capacity to bring healing is awe-inspiring. How can one person find a cure for polio, while another is busy devising laws that prevent people from marrying because their skin colors are different? How can Mother Teresa and Adolf Hitler both have been of the human race?"

Beatrice nodded, clearing her throat. "And why does God allow it?" she added, back to a whisper.

"The great problem of evil, which haunts the world..."

Beatrice gazed at her friend, waiting, barely breathing.

"Dear heart, if I had solved that paradox, I would be canonized – or *at least* more people would read my articles!... Evil is a mystery, but I think sometimes we give it too much power. In no way am I belittling any of the countless people who have suffered down the ages. Still, evil is not equal and opposite to good. It is altogether lesser than, and it does not have the final say." – Anna took a long sip of whisky and blushed slightly. "I'm probably not expressing myself well," she went on. "Many of these thoughts have lived in my own head for so long, emerging slowly from things I've read and experienced, and till now I haven't articulated them to another soul. It is all a mystery, and one I don't believe we will fully unravel in this lifetime, so I hesitate to make sweeping statements about it."

Food came, and for a few minutes conversation paused. Somehow Beatrice was always famished when she got to The Blue Ball Inn, which was good, as portions were hearty.

"I do think, though," Anna continued, setting down her knife and fork, "that, when considering theodicy, it is nigh impossible to overestimate the importance of Christ as the Suffering Servant who enters into the human condition – who suffers *with*, as well as *for* us, so that we need never be alone in our own suffering."

Beatrice nodded again.

"As to your other... objection?" Anna paused, smiling, "the banality of so much of our day-to-day lives? I think that is a problem of 'seeing but never perceiving, hearing but never understanding.' To paraphrase Coleridge, the world is an inexhaustible treasure, but the film of familiarity blinds us to it. There," she concluded, "my sermon is done, and I'm buying the next round."

*

A musty smell of old books mingled with the eternal damp pervading the downstairs of her parents' house. Beatrice thought it must be the salt always heavy on the air, seeping into everything. The backdoor stood open onto a lawn, and lush smells of fresh-cut grass and gardenia drifted in on the breeze. She inhaled deeply, before passing into the 'library', where so many familiar friends from her youth resided on shelves or sat in haphazard stacks on the floor. *Treasure Island, The Scarlet Pimpernel, Nancy Drew...*

There was something as soothing as an embrace about entering a room full of books, especially if some of them were old. The scent, the silence full of latent words just waiting to be read, of whole worlds waiting to be discovered or revisited... There were literary characters from her childhood whom Beatrice still thought of as friends – almost in the way that she recalled actual friends from her grammar school days, whom she hadn't seen since.

That same summer after her year abroad, Beatrice joined her college friends Hannah and Louisa for a road trip up the coast to Big Sur. They hiked late the day they arrived because there was such a vast wilderness to be seen and so little time in which to see it. Shadows sloped across the valley their trail traced; the sun touched a far granite peak with its final, tangerine rays. Alpenglow – what a magical-sounding word! The moon floated above the far end of the valley, not yet full, but almost too bright to be believed.

The next morning they were tired and a little sore, but set out again, thirsting for more beauty. As they climbed, the world fell away below in cascades of sunny wild yarrow and gnarled manzanita, sloping steeply down to the Pacific. To the left pine trees, like regiments of soldiers, marched in orderly rows toward the sea. Fog eddied and crept among the towering redwoods, cold fingers refusing to release their grasp entirely, despite a July sun overhead. The fog, whenever they walked through it, had almost the effect of snow, producing a profound quiet, occasionally interrupted by crashing waves far below or a woodpecker or Steller's jay crying from a branch above.

To the right, the sea blanketed much of the view, blue and immense, with now and then a whale or dolphin spouting to remind you of the vast other world beneath the surface. Directly before them, a thousand feet below, the water was a color so vivid it seemed to defy naming. It belonged in a tropical paradise with hot, white beaches and palms; yet here they were, looking at the cold waters of Big Sur and there *it* was, sparkling back at them in brilliant aquamarine.

The next stretch of trail was heavily overgrown, with blackberry vines and poison oak tendrils reaching out from one side, while wild raspberries brushed at them from the other. Sagebrush scented the faint breeze along with a spicy note of pine, and as the sun strengthened the air felt heavy, as if they were indeed in an island rainforest.

That evening the warmth of good fellowship enveloped them like a blanket. A rustle of burning logs in the cabin's stone fireplace, the fog-shrouded land-and-seascape without, as well as a ready supply of red wine in their glasses, all added to a general sense of well-being arising from a good meal and conversation. Times like these came like fermatas in one's life, offering a chance to pause, to be still and really savor the people one so enjoyed but too often took for granted in the press of ordinary days.

Later that summer, Beatrice and her friends travelled up into the Sierra Nevadas. There was a quality to the freshness of the mountain air – a cold, crisp sweetness – that washed over your senses like a baptism. The exhalations of pines, smoke from recent fires, late summer rain, ripe apples... Charred trees still clung savagely to the wasted foothills where flames had torn through the previous year. But faintly – ever so faintly – a blush of new growth had begun to cover the exposed ridges and ravines, like a woman drawing a mantle over her naked body.

*

Beatrice could not forget the first time she'd laid eyes on Patrick. She was back home at last, wrestling with her twin desires to be a nun and to pursue music. Mother, meanwhile, kept trying to introduce her to boys. They *were* only boys: Beatrice knew what a man was like – she had a perfect example in Dad. Even her brothers were well on their way to becoming men. But these specimens…

She shut her book with a snap. It was hot and she wanted another dip in the water. As part of her efforts to avoid more of Mother's well-intentioned match-making, she had taken up sunbathing just beyond Scripps Pier – a healthy distance from the Club. It was a quietish weekday morning, and she'd thought she had this particular strip of beach to herself, so she was surprised, as she waded into the water, to notice a surfer on the near side of the pier. A little annoyed, too.

He rode a wave in and nearly knocked her down before diving off his board at the last minute. Standing up, he spewed salt water, a rainbow of droplets falling from his long curly hair. Beatrice felt her outrage faltering at the sight of his muscular physique. And she'd never before seen a person so tan with such blue eyes… *Beatrice!* She shook herself. He had behaved very rudely and should be made to own up to it.

"Sorry, didn't see you there!" he called over.

"I hope not!" She balled her fists to hold onto her anger.

He squinted across the bright water. "Oh, you're mad."

"You almost decapitated me!"

He threw his head back and laughed.

She was aware she was being melodramatic, but he shouldn't be laughing about it.

After a moment, he said, "Don't worry, I'm a pretty good surfer. You were never in danger, even though I didn't see you till the last minute."

"You're not that good." – She didn't know why she said it.

"Oh, you're a surfer, are you?"

"I am."

"Really?" – He looked half incredulous, and half curious.

"If you don't believe me, give me your board."

He swept a bow and passed her his surfboard. She grabbed it and paddled out, feeling some combination of irate, foolish and intoxicated with this strange man.

The first wave she hesitated too long over and it swelled past her. She could feel her heartbeat moving into her throat as she waited. No, this was no way to do it! She closed her eyes and waited for her breath to steady. Another decent swell rose and she paddled for it. The moment a wave began to propel you forward gave such a feeling of oneness with nature – she loved to lose herself in it. Beatrice scrambled to her feet and glided in.

The waves here were smallish this morning, and she was beginning to feel that she'd overreacted to this handsome surfer by the time she returned his board to him. He was waiting for her in the shallows, expression stunned, so she forgot her contrition. This was deeply satisfying.

"Clearly you didn't believe me," she said.

They walked shoreward as though it had been discussed.

"It's not often I get to see a woman who can surf." – He eyed her with admiration.

"Well," she dropped onto the warm sand, pretending to adjust her bikini to avoid looking into his so-blue eyes, "my dad shapes surfboards as a hobby, so really I didn't have much of a choice!"

"Okay, now I have to meet your dad." – He chuckled. "On the list of 'things I never thought I'd say to a woman' that ranks pretty high!"

They both laughed this time. She liked how it felt, laughing with him. They sat and talked until the sun passed its zenith, at which point Beatrice regretfully acknowledged that she was starving; he agreed. Squinting at the waves, she worked up the courage to say the next thing she'd been thinking. Getting the words out was always the hardest part.

"I'm sure you could come over for lunch... if you wanted to meet my dad, I mean." She hastened to add that, since it was a Saturday, he was likely to be home.

"I'd like that."

"There's usually just sandwiches and salad but..."

"I'm sure it's better than what I'd be eating if I went home for lunch."

They walked through Kellogg Park and past the Sea Lodge, skirted the Club and made their way along Paseo Dorado to her parents' house. His eyes widened slightly as she turned in at their driveway, but he followed gamely, surfboard and all.

Beatrice hadn't fallen for a man in some time – maybe ever, if she really thought about it. She had erected a fence around her affections, in part out of conviction that she should be a nun, in part for reasons less clear to herself. Men seemed safer as friends, with everyone's emotions pigeonholed.

She set about thus to pigeonhole Patrick, but just when she thought she'd been successful, he presented some new aspect that she had not accounted for or assailed her from some fresh quarter. Her parents took to him immediately, and Mother soon began asking with a gleam in her eye, "How's Patrick?" It was irritating, but no more so than Beatrice's own reactions to him.

One example. They were walking along the Beach Club's esplanade one night, and in her typical clumsy fashion she tripped over an unseen lip in the pavement. Patrick grabbed her to keep her from falling, and her heart fluttered like a moth's wings against a lamp as he held onto her for a second longer than was strictly necessary.

Her brothers liked surfing with Patrick, so even once she'd resolved to see him less and stopped suggesting activities to do together, he would appear at the house for post-surfing breakfasts. Sometimes he materialized, apparently at their invitation, even when no surfing was involved.

She came upstairs, for example, one gray Saturday morning to a mass of guys in the kitchen where usually there were none, unless Dad was making his famous lobster bisque. Eva, their live-in maid/cook, was expostulating to Beatrice's brother Will as he tried to pour pancake batter and splattered a good deal of it over the range. On second take, there weren't actually so many people in the room, it just felt crowded when all except Eva and Beatrice were tall, broad-shouldered and deep-voiced. Beatrice wove among them, half-awake, searching for the coffee pot, and was just turning to reach for a mug when she smacked into Patrick's chest. She stumbled backwards, dazed and rubbing her face, half-hearing his apologies and her brothers' knowing laughter.

She'd thought about this witching effect he had on her. Was it his scent? his voice? his eyes? Whatever the answer, she took a long moment before reassuring him that she was okay – so much so that he put a hand on her shoulder as if in concern, which only added to her befuddlement.

She slipped out onto the balcony with her coffee. The day was mild, despite overcast skies, and a soothing medley of lawn-mowing and tennis ball volleys carried across from the Club. She tucked her feet underneath her and leaned back in an Adirondack chair, inhaling tangy notes of coffee mingled with the ever-present salt in the air. She closed her eyes.

"Quite the view."

Beatrice jumped. Patrick was looking at *her* but inclined his head toward the red roofs of the Club, its gangly palms and luxuriant bougainvilleas, with gray-blue ocean beyond.

"Yes." – It was true, though she often took the vista for granted. It was also all she trusted herself to say, her stomach doing cartwheels and her hands feeling unsteady.

Seeing her life through Patrick's eyes, Beatrice felt a discomfort she'd pushed to the back of her mind for years. She adhered to a radical creed that exalted the poor and warned against the snares of wealth; yet here she was spending the summer at her parents' ocean-view home, complete with live-in help, across the street from a private club where she could swim, play tennis or surf whenever the fancy took her. She never encountered a person suffering hunger or want without going out of her way to do so.

Beatrice stared at the ring on her hand, which her parents had given her for a recent birthday. She studied its golden band inlaid with tiny diamonds and wondered what the answer was. She didn't think she ought to throw the gift in her parents' faces; they seemed to have derived such joy from giving it to her – no harm in a few luxuries, surely? Now, however, she wondered if she could continue on as she had, enjoying herself with blinders on, struggling now and then in her privileged quandary of which path to take in life.

She resolved to ask the priest about helping with his soup kitchen this Sunday after church. At least it would be a step in the right direction.

Meanwhile, Patrick said: "You've been avoiding me."

It was a statement, not an accusation or yet a question.

Beatrice stared north. Below golden cliffs, a few glints of light played on the water where the sun was burning through morning cloud cover. "Have you ever felt like you knew exactly what you were supposed to do with your life?" she asked, turning her face to him.

He settled into a chair beside her: "I'm not sure I have."

"The first time, I was little – seven, maybe – and I had my first piano recital. I'm sure I wasn't any good, but I felt like a butterfly finally spreading its wings. I knew then, that was what I was *supposed* to do – or, so I thought. Then, in college, I 'got religion', as my family likes to say."

She felt the weight of his eyes, colored like the sea where the light touched it, even though she wasn't looking at him.

"And I felt – I feel..." Strange how she spoke almost as if she'd changed her mind once again, "drawn to a life in a convent or religious order."

He guffawed loudly, and she looked up, cheeks hot, to see him first shocked, then struggling to recompose his face. "I'm sorry – I – I didn't think you were serious."

Beatrice hesitated between indignation and an alarming need to forgive him. While she vacillated, to her further surprise, he began to quote Alexander Pope:

> "How happy is the blameless vestal's lot!
> The world forgetting, by the world forgot.
> Eternal sunshine of the spotless mind,
> Each prayer accepted and each wish resigned."

The words held her in their lovely web, suspended by gossamer threads. But was he mocking her, quoting *Eloisa to Abelard*? As she remembered it, the sad, twisted story of passion, rage and heartbreak ended with *forced* exile into holy orders for her and castration for him.

"To be honest," he spoke tentatively, "I didn't even know you were Catholic."

"I'm not."

He ran both of his hands through his gold-tipped hair, a gesture that never failed to make her wish that she could do the same. "Okay..."

She dragged her mind back to the conversation. "There are Anglican religious orders. I learned about them when I was studying in Cambridge."

"I see. So you will either be a musician or a nun. Which means... you can't associate with me?"

"I – you know what I mean."

He just looked at her, and she realized he was going to make her say it. She barely knew what 'it' was. She had so far successfully avoided articulating 'it' to herself.

"I –" her throat felt cottony.

"Hey Patrick, come get some pancakes." – He was then almost bodily dragged back inside, and she felt both relieved and deflated as she finished her coffee alone.

"You thought I'd let you get away with banishing me, without even the courtesy of an explanation?"

Beatrice scuffed a sneaker in the dirt, wishing for an earthquake to swallow her before she had to answer.

Her parents' last-minute decision to visit their country cousins in San Luis Obispo had seemed like the perfect opportunity to get away from Patrick without further excuse, until her brothers got the bright idea to invite him along to surf the colder waters of Pismo Beach and Morro Bay. She was deeply angry with them, with Patrick and with herself for caring so much. This stretch of coast had always felt a little Edenic to her; now it was being invaded by someone who turned her ordered world back into a sea of chaos.

How well she remembered coming here as a child; the flavors and smells took her back as soon as she arrived, particularly in summer. The pleasures of summer fruit when you're young are as riotous and decadent as the most indulgent of La Jolla society parties might be to an adult. The season started with berries: raspberries and blackberries, boysenberries and olallieberries staining your fingers and tongue as you ate half again as many as you put in your basket. Then came the cherries, purple-black ones and sunset gold and red ones, sweet and tart and plump. Next were the plums, perhaps Beatrice's favorite, with the word 'plummy' so suiting the fruit's color and taste as to make it a kind of onomatopoeia of the senses. Around that time too came the strange but delightful yellowy-green plumcots, with the same dusky white film on their skins that plums had, and of course apricots, with skin soft as a baby's bottom. Maybe those were her favorite – at least until the peaches and nectarines arrived.

Vegetable harvests were less delightful to a child's taste-buds, though it was still exciting to pull up long, fingery carrots webbed with damp earth or to dig for potatoes. It had all been unfamiliar and exotic for Beatrice and her siblings in those early summers, given that they otherwise had so little to do with the soil, being rather children of sand and seawater. Each summer from the time she was nine or so, they would drive the long stretches of highway up to San Luis Obispo to stay at their cousins', often with Mother and Dad then travelling elsewhere.

A white dirt road led out through cow pastures past a creek lined with gnarled sycamores to a hilltop where their aunt and uncle's farmhouse stood, surrounded by fruit trees and grape and berry vines. They would be welcomed by a cacophony of dogs barking, hens furiously flapping out of the way of the station wagon and kids running out of the barn or scrambling down from trees to greet them.

Their aunt (well, technically she was Mother's cousin, but they'd grown up calling them Aunt Liz and Uncle Bill) always had supper on in the kitchen, and they would hover briefly around a delectable smell of cobbler from the oven before running off to the creek, which dwindled to a stream after spring rains, to hunt for frogs, or out to the barn to see the newest litter of mousers. After dinner, everyone would sit out on the wide porch, soaking in the mellow warmth of evening and watching a trout-silver moon rise over the rusty mountains behind them as Uncle Bill told some story of his years as a park ranger while sipping whiskey.

Beatrice would sit on a porch step, leaning her head against her dad's leg, picturing the lonely expanses Uncle Bill described patrolling, spreading his bedroll beneath a brilliant canopy of stars, hearing a distant wolf's howl and making sure his pistol was close to hand. After Mother and Dad had left (usually the morning following their arrival), a month of days would commence that Beatrice was always reminded of when she read *Fern Hill*:

And honoured among wagons I was prince of the apple towns
And once below a time I lordly had the trees and leaves
Trail with daisies and barley
Down the rivers of the windfall light.

One of the things young Beatrice loved most during this period was inventing new worlds for herself and her brothers and cousins. Endless adventures could be had and countless characters inhabited. They would revisit the realms of their favorite stories, becoming the Pevensie children's long-lost siblings or Frodo's trusty companions, who defied witches or fought orcs as the fancy took them. As they grew older, the stories would change, from Robin Hood and knights in armor to marines like Dad had been, fighting on the beachheads of Pacific islands. Beatrice fit herself in naturally, not bothering about the anachronism of a girl as outlaw in Sherwood Forest when she didn't feel like playing Maid Marian.

The world had been an enchanted place for them, and it was never difficult to imagine among the emerald greens and amethyst purples of summer grasses and wildflowers, when they ventured into the Sierras, that fairies really did haunt the meadows; or, on their first visit to a black-as-pitch mountain cave, that a dragon could be lurking at its furthest depths, standing guard over piles of corrupt and corrupting treasure.

These games of make-believe were how they passed the time with their cousins – what time was not taken up with chores or eating fresh fruit. Often they used these stories to make their chores go by faster. They would all be weeding and sweating under a Saturday morning sun, and Beatrice (usually) would begin to narrate, piloting them out of the vegetable garden of here-and-now to lands of long ago and far away.

Eventually Mother and Dad would return from their peregrinations to pick up Beatrice and her brothers and take them home, promising the usual exchange over Christmas, when the country cousins would come down to La Jolla for bouts of surfing and fishing...

But Patrick was now here on the farm with all of them, and it was impossible for Beatrice to hide from him when they were meant to be friends. After a day of failing to avoid one another, followed by a few stilted conversations, he proposed they take a walk.

They meandered away from the farmhouse a short distance. In the end, their feet took them to a lone sycamore that grew apart from its fellows, its roots deep enough to find residual water from the stream a few hundred yards away.

The tree's trunk bent to such a perfect angle that they were able to sit on it. Without really knowing how it happened, Beatrice realized as she looked up to answer some comment of Patrick's that they were sitting very close indeed; she tried to shift, and her shoulder grazed his. She could feel a thickness in the air, as though their unspoken longings were bridging the scant empty space between them. Their eyes met and she felt her own widen. The words she'd meant to say caught on her tongue, but she did not look away. They teetered on the cusp of time and other things. Then he leaned in, catching her chin with his finger, and kissed her.

She backed away in surprise. Then, as though drawn by iron bands, she reached out and pulled him toward her.

Minutes later, they were looking at one another as though for the first time. He reached for her hand, and she held his gingerly, as if she were handling a grenade. Her mind was racing so fast she couldn't catch a single thought. She was afraid to meet his eyes again, yet she wanted nothing more.

Someone's footsteps padded down the dirt road, and she withdrew her hand instinctively. A shadow skittered across Patrick's face and was gone. He stood up, shoving his hands into the back pockets of his Levi's, and moved a little space away. Her youngest cousin Henry had come to summon them to dinner and was blissfully unaware he was intruding on their tête-à-tête.

*

California always felt different in the rain than other places. Colorado had impromptu summer showers, pelting down, then vanishing as swiftly as they came in a glory of snowy clouds and cerulean skies. England seemed almost indifferent to rain, as though a steady spitting was its natural state of being and interludes of sunshine a rare intrusion from some other realm. But here, a late October rain came in the night and you could feel the earth breathe a sigh of gratitude. Along with the intoxicating scent of damp soil, you could smell eucalyptus, sage and verbena. Every leaf held beads of rainwater like rare jewels. After perhaps a gray morning, the sun would blaze back and the landscape take on a luminous quality under skies racing with rent clouds. A walk near the coast would get your heart racing too, as the storm surge would have reshaped the beach, and the waves pounded the breakwaters, piers and cliffs with awesome power.

On one such afternoon, Patrick appeared on the doorstep of the bungalow Beatrice shared with two college friends who, like her, couldn't quite bring themselves to 1) decide what to do with their lives or 2) leave San Luis. It wasn't, in Beatrice's case anyway, that she was nostalgic for her college years. But this place had gotten into her blood. Even La Jolla, with its exotic beauty, paled in comparison. Especially as you got to the northern stretches of the county's coastline, the beauty here was far more raw.

Perhaps her love of it had begun with those visits to their cousins' farm in childhood, but San Luis felt like her own now. And here was Patrick, who complicated *everything*, yet made it better, refusing apparently to let sleeping dogs lie.

"Oh!" she said, though they'd been standing there staring at one another for what seemed like many minutes, "would you like to come in?"

Beatrice awoke the morning after with a battle in her chest. One half of her felt the full weight of what she'd done: she'd surrendered so eagerly what she had been taught all her life to protect. The heaviness of disappointed expectations was almost unbearable. And yet... there was also a strange buoyancy, a deep well-spring of life that had been unstopped and was now bubbling up inside her. She ricocheted from anguish to ebullience and back again until she thought she might lose her mind – or blurt out what had happened between her and Patrick to her housemates. Instead, she decided to go for a long walk alone.

The beeches and cottonwoods and sycamores were yellow torches, and a confetti of fallen leaves strewed the ground. A gust of wind, carrying more leaves and a smattering of rain, flung its weight at her, then rushed by. Though at first she had dreaded going out in the elements, she was now relishing the weather; being in the midst of wind and rain made her feel somehow more open to the full inrush of life as it happened, moment to moment, as wild and unpredictable and exhilarating as the storm. She breathed in deeply, letting the sensation wash over her. The air was sweet and chill; gray clouds cloaked the sky and others massed purple-black above hills to her left. Everywhere she looked was a revelation.

The entire affair had been so unpremeditated, and slightly wine-infused, that neither she nor Patrick had thought about birth control until after the deed was done. Only then did he ask, assuming her affirmative response, and when she gave a negative, they both laughed nervously and told each other the odds weren't *that* high. She hadn't even admitted to him in the moment that this was her first time, not wanting to give him pause. She might tell him when they met later for dinner.

Meanwhile, she tried to remember what she'd learned about the female reproductive system in biology class. Her parents had been shy on the subject of sex, though Mother had given her a very prim version of 'the talk' after Beatrice had her first period. They had been shopping for summer hats when it happened. Beatrice had started to feel an unfamiliar twist in her lower stomach. At first, she'd barely noticed, but as they'd walked into a second shop she began to feel worse, and by the time the lady was offering her hats to try on she was wishing very much to be at home in bed.

She hated making a scene, so she'd waited as long as she could stand to tell Mother that she felt sick. She kept hoping it would go away, but it didn't, and when Mother asked her point blank what was wrong, she nearly burst into tears.

Back home she'd lain down for a bit, but the pain had persisted. Her parents, she could tell, were starting to worry, and when she went to the bathroom she knew they were right to be concerned: there was a silver dollar-sized patch of blood on her underwear. Her heart was in her throat as she went to tell Mother. But instead of telling Dad to get the car and drive them to the hospital, Mother simply smiled (if Beatrice hadn't had infinite faith in her mother's kindness, she would have suspected she was trying not to laugh) and told her it was not dangerous. In fact, it was a wonderful thing. This was the beginning of her becoming a woman.

Beatrice had not been impressed. If this was how it began, how would it continue? No tales of damsels in distress and knights in shining armor had included *this*! Looking back, she smiled at her younger self's naiveté. But there was part of her who missed that little girl. And, in a way, she'd surrendered the last part of her only twelve hours ago.

Beatrice could sense herself sliding into a sinkhole of panic. Conversations ricocheted around her as she walked through the house in a breathless daze. Somehow she had let Patrick persuade her to come to his *parents'* for Thanksgiving – despite the fact that the two of them had really only been on one or two proper dates. She felt every eye on her was not simply observing, but ferreting out her secret.

She retraced her steps once more to the kitchen, where the women of the family – Patrick's mother Paula, grandmother (introduced only as Gammy) and sister Beth were all hard at work. Beatrice wanted to offer to help but feared any task they gave her might reveal her ignorance. Had Patrick told them her mother had a maid who did the cooking?

Patrick found her hovering in the doorway. He slid a hand around her waist and leaned in to kiss her. She batted him away: "Your mother – your *grandmother*, Patrick!"

He drew her closer against him.

Suddenly – was it the turkey Beth was retrieving from the oven? or the thought of what Patrick would say when he learned? – a wave of nausea swept over Beatrice and she felt her skin slicken with sweat.

"Sweetheart!" – Patrick turned her toward him. His face blanched as he saw hers. "Let's go sit you down."

She nodded, lips pressed together and hands in fists, willing herself to breathe slowly and on no account to vomit in the Woodings' kitchen. Patrick half-led, half-carried her to the den where his father was watching the game with Beth's husband (whose name eluded her), while their kids were upstairs napping. Both men were both so engrossed that they didn't notice anything was wrong, which suited Beatrice very well. Patrick left her for a moment and returned with a damp cloth for her forehead and a glass of cold water. Kneeling by her side, he watched as she sipped carefully.

"How do you feel? Any better?" – He ran a hand along each of her arms, as though searching for signs.

She nodded, afraid if she said anything she would burst into tears. Her lip quivered rebelliously.

"What's wrong?"

She glanced at his father and brother-in-law, both staring at the television. He caught her meaning:

"Let's go get some fresh air."

She nodded again and stood, with assistance. He grabbed their parkas and held the door for her.

The view from the deck took her breath. They'd arrived late the previous night, and she hadn't ventured out since. The sun hung in a cloudless sky, and she felt its rays filtering through the towering firs that surrounded the cabin on three sides. Where she and Patrick stood looking out, the trees were kept at bay to preserve a view of the mountains across the valley. Sheer faces of granite were lined with snow wherever a rare ledge jutted out or lone tree ventured to grow.

The tail end of the storm had lingered long enough to make the drive up here twice as long as it should have been, between putting on chains and going slow as they chattered under the wheels. Now, looking out at the other-worldly landscape, Beatrice realized it all had been worth it.

It took her back to trips to the snow in her childhood. Waking up so early you felt sick, but still tried to force down some cereal, then everyone piling into the station wagon to traverse long, flat roads through the Mojave that began after a time to climb imperceptibly alongside the Sierra Nevadas... The drive up was a (mostly) silent battle between middle and back-seaters. No one knew why this had to be, but the rules of siblinghood were inscrutable, and there was no point in questioning them. Competition over snacks, control of the windows and general harassment of one another all went on as quietly as possible, so as not to attract attention from the front. Everyone hoped not to have to stop to put on chains in the finger-biting cold on the final ascent to Mammoth. The pines' scent and crunch of snow underfoot never ceased to stir their spirits, even as they shivered in their jeans and pulled on parkas, piling out of the back to help unload skis and bags. The cold air had its own smell, crusty and fresh, as they hauled their gear up to adjoining rooms at Mammoth Mountain Inn and Dad went to get everyone lift tickets...

Patrick helped her into her coat, then shrugged into his. He rested his hands lightly on her waist, and she pulled them around her, leaning back into his warmth as they stared out at a freshly recreated world. The silence between them was easy, peaceful. She let herself be embraced by it, pushing to the back of her mind the question of how things might change once she had told him.

"Feeling better?" he asked.

She nodded. This was the moment; but she waited a little, savoring the view and the quiet as a *we* for perhaps a last time. The lump in her throat grew to feel truly suffocating, and she sensed her earlier nausea returning. "Patrick, I..." she swallowed quickly to keep her emotions (and breakfast) down, "I need to tell you –" she could feel tears start to squeeze out at the corners of her eyes.

"Beatrice, what?" – He pulled away to face her. "You're scaring me. You can't possibly intend to break up with me at my parents' cabin *on* Thanksgiving Day!"

"No, I –" she laughed thickly, "not that. If anything, you..." she dropped her voice to an involuntary whisper, "might be the one breaking up with me."

His expression was incredulous.

Out with it, Beatrice.

"I'm –" she gulped, reminding herself it was true; saying it would make it no more so. "I'm pregnant." *There.*

For a moment he seemed frozen. Then, such a wave of shock washed over his face that she was compelled to add:

"It's yours – of course."

He still said nothing, and her body chilled with a wholly different kind of cold that started at her heart and radiated out. She put a hand on the railing to support herself.

This seemed to rouse him. He moved toward her again, saying as he did: "I know. I mean, I would never doubt that, Beatrice," as though no time had passed between her words and his. He put out a hand and tucked a strand of her hair behind one ear.

Relief at having told him and his taking it (so far) so well turned the trickle of tears into a torrent, and for a moment she could do nothing but cling to him, her face in his jacket and sobs shaking her body. At last her tears subsided, and she looked up, eyes hot and nose dripping:

"Now what?"

"Well, I guess we better get married." – He said it so matter-of-factly, so easily, that she laughed aloud.

"Really?"

"Well, unless you don't want to." For the first time since learning that he was going to be a father, he seemed unsure.

A thought struck her like a blow: "But I'd finally decided to give my life to the Church!"

He chuckled. "Not yet you aren't." Then, eyes averted: "I mean – unless – I assumed you wouldn't want –" He seemed reluctant to finish his thought.

After a pause, she realized what he wasn't saying.

"Oh no, I – I just *couldn't*. You don't want me to, do you?" she asked, now preparing for a fight.

"No! And I didn't think that you would. But I know your dreams aren't really for a woman who's with child. Or with children in tow." – A thought seemed to strike him. "Are you sure you're – have you seen a doctor yet?"

"No, but..." she blushed. It was strange to be discussing this so frankly with a man she had never intended to kiss in the first place. Well, that wasn't right exactly. She had more or less resolved not to kiss *any* man as she moved closer towards her embrace of a monastic life, but somehow he had crept into her heart... She realized he was waiting for an answer while she stood ruminating.

"I – ah..." She took a deep breath and said it all in one go. "My cycle is very regular and I'm two weeks late and starting to feel sick..." She could feel her cheeks heating up again. "I only put it all together this morning. But yes, I'm sure." She felt her flush deepen. "I don't know *what* my parents will say. It's not the sort of thing we do." – She hovered on the brink between laughter and tears. She thought she caught a flash of concern at the mention of "parents". For his own? hers?

But he gathered her up tight in his arms and said: "Let's think about that later. Tomorrow we can drive into Nevada and get married." – She caught her breath at the coolness with which he mentioned it again, but he carried on: "Then maybe the rest of the weekend can be a sort of honeymoon before we go back to jobs and doctors and housing and..." he swallowed, "parenthood."

Her heart clenched with dismay. For several years now she had been quietly resolved not to marry. Besides, one had standards. All her girlish dreams of romance (taken in large part from the pages of Jane Austen, L. M. Montgomery and the Brontës) cried out against marrying a man she wasn't *violently* in love with.

She could hardly deny that she was starting to feel something resembling love for Patrick, or she would never have found herself star-gazing on Perfumo Crest that fateful night a month before. No, it was fruitless to protest that she was not falling in love; still, it was far from the poetic court-ship she had dreamed of. Shame that was an almost physical weight pressed on her chest every time she thought about what had happened under a blanket of frosty white stars. Soon people would suspect that their sudden marriage – if marry they must – was a feeble attempt to cover over the fact that she was already with child. *I'm* Lydia *Bennet*, she realized in horror. Having spent half a life imagining herself to be the witty, incisive and unimpeachable older sister Lizzy, this smarted deeply.

Prior to her now-irrelevant decision to become a nun, Beatrice had always thought she'd have a gradual build-up to parenthood, if she experienced it at all. First, could she feed herself and pay bills on her own? Check. Next, could she keep a dog alive? Check. Then maybe, someday, when her position as a renowned composer was established, she might revisit the family question. Instead, everything had been turned on its head. A wave of bitterness surged in her; there were plenty of women who longed in vain for what had happened to her. How could she have been so foolish, and what would she tell her parents? – If only she hadn't skipped the own-a-dog step, she would have someone close at hand to comfort her now, without the need for explanations.

The love of a dog was, in he mind, perhaps the most generous, disinterested love one could witness: forgiving to a fault, tirelessly loyal, never withholding its affection. The love of a parent was of course deeper and more sacrificial, but rare was the parent who – though they surely loved their child regardless – did not expect a return for their labors, whether in grandchildren, help in old age or just time and attention. Certainly these did not seem like unreasonable expectations (although, had events transpired differently, Beatrice might not have produced any grandchildren for her own parents). But a dog simply loves, in a way that, though it sounded close to heretical, Beatrice could not help thinking was reminiscent of the dog's Creator. A love so lavish does not demand a response, though it will always welcome one.

She remembered Dad crying when their white-muzzled lab, Lucy, had died. Lucy had been fourteen, a good age for a big dog and a year or two older than Beatrice herself at the time. She had died while they were on a family vacation in Baja, simply not waking up one morning when she was usually sniffing around early in anticipation of breakfast. They buried her there, placing a driftwood cross over her grave, which overlooked a bay and beach where she had loved to run.

When they returned home to La Jolla, Beatrice and her brothers had spent a couple of weeks red-eyed and mopey as they kept running across Lucy's favorite toy or last bone. Then one Saturday, Dad declared that that was enough and ordered them all into the car. They drove northeast, to where ranches sprawled under towering eucalyptus trees. Dad pulled onto a dirt drive that reminded Beatrice of her cousins', and a man in a cowboy hat waved them towards a big, weathered barn.

Motes had drifted through the shafts of sunlight piercing the dimness. Smells of hay and horse manure enveloped them as they followed the man. The horse stalls were empty, and the whole place still save for a couple of swallows that darted out of the dark over their heads. Beatrice thought she heard a tiny cry, and the rancher pushed open the door to the last stall; it was lined with fresh hay, and in the back a golden retriever lay on her side, slowly thumping her tail in welcome as they peered in. It took a moment to see that she wasn't alone. Eight little yellow balls of fluff nuzzled at her stomach, or snuffled around their makeshift home, sometimes whining softly when they got lost on their way back to mother.

"Would you like to hold one?"

None of the children had said anything, just nodded vigorously, and the rancher scooped up one puppy after another for them to get acquainted with. Half the time he grabbed them by the scruff of the neck, which Beatrice was worried about until she saw that the puppies didn't mind. She'd felt a surge of love as the pup she held against her nestled into her arms, licking her face when she pulled it close enough for it to reach with its little pink tongue.

"Should we take one home?" Dad asked.

They all nodded at that, although Beatrice felt a twinge of guilt remembering poor Lucy. Her throat tightened and she looked away for a moment, blinking rapidly. Dad seemed to get it, for he put a hand on her shoulder. They stood that way for some minutes, the pup in her arms still licking her with abandon while the boys debated which one to choose.

Coming home for Christmas had always been one of Beatrice's great joys since she'd first moved away for college. Now that she and Patrick had been apart, though married-at-a-distance, for nearly a month, she missed him hungrily. Although she was far from sure that it had been the 'right' choice, she had to admit that she longed for the moment she could touch his face and have him take her hand again.

At the same time, though her belly was not protruding noticeably yet (she checked in the mirror daily with a mix of anticipation and dread), her stomach still turned loathingly at many foods. She didn't know how she would get through Christmas dinner or all the family meals before and after.

While she tried not to give away her condition, they had to tell her family they were married, and had been since late November. Mother would be so disappointed at missing the opportunity to throw her only daughter a big wedding, but would she suspect why? Would Dad approve of Patrick regardless? He had welcomed him in summer as a friend of hers and the boys, but this was different, to say the least.

Beatrice missed the sense of wellbeing she had felt in childhood, snuggled down under the covers, lights out and her siblings in bed too, but one lamp still on in the hall and a murmur of trustworthy voices drifting down from upstairs. It was just a splash of light on a picture-hung wall and a half-audible conversation between Mother and Dad, but it had anchored her whole world and left her with a sense, as she drifted to sleep, that there was peace on earth.

Now she drove south on a sunlit, 65° day. Mornings and nights had grown chilly, but days were still pleasant enough to leave the windows down. The ocean raced her as she drove the stretch of coast from Goleta to Ventura; palms, hills and beach towns folded together; freeway overpasses and high-rise buildings loomed up as she entered Los Angeles.

Beatrice had hoped to see Patrick before she got home, but when she called his apartment, he didn't answer. No doubt he was caught up after a lecture. Sometimes she still thought it was funny that the guy she had pegged as a surfer bum was also a newly minted professor of literature, embarking on a teaching career at UCSD. No wonder the man could quote Pablo Neruda until she felt her whole body blush. He'd written her recently with lines from a sonnet:

I love you as the plant that doesn't bloom but carries
The light of those flowers, hidden, within itself...

She listened to his phone ring and ring with no answer. She felt exposed in a phone booth on the main drag in Encinitas and her stomach felt hollow, though she'd just eaten. A thought flitted at the back of her head: *What if he's changed* his *mind?* – Either way, it was time to go home.

She took the coastal route past Del Mar racetrack and up Torrey Pines hill, and soon turned down towards La Jolla Shores. Her heart warmed despite her fears as she drove along Avenida de la Playa, its shop entrances festooned with Christmas lights and patrons walking about in beachwear.

She arrived earlier than she'd estimated, and everyone was out. It was Eva's day off so, after letting herself in, she poked around in the fridge for a snack (she was amazed to find she was hungry again) before browsing through the house to admire Mother's exuberant decorations. A collection of nutcrackers was prominent, including one the size of a toddler standing beside the fireplace. Mistletoe, stockings, garlands, poinsettias and of course a big tree...

Beatrice settled in a corner of the couch and stared at the nativity on the coffee-table – one of many nativities scattered around the house, all of which had their rightful place. In this one Mary's face, so calm in white porcelain, was far from how Beatrice imagined the actual Mother of God to look: olive-skinned, bearing a weight of judgement from her family and others in her community who knew her secret – a child, and one whom, heaven only knew, would not merely interrupt her meager plans for her own life, but would disrupt the smug plans of rulers and emperors...

An angel had appeared with a shocking announcement, and Mary said: "Let it be to me according to your word." Didn't she have questions, aside from the 'how'? protests, even? "Why not that girl down the street? She's in need of a little humbling." No. Though Mary had retreated to her cousin's house for a time, perhaps to gather strength for her anticipated disgrace, the first thing she'd said upon arriving was: "My soul magnifies the Lord, and my spirit rejoices in God my Savior." Well did Beatrice remember the Magnificat from Evensong at Clare College. It was a great manifesto of revolutionary justice, at a time when Mary might have been excused for getting cold feet about surprise parenthood, let alone this whole *theotokos* concept...

Beatrice got up and walked to the mantel. There, in addition to another nativity, were the family portraits through the years that Mother always insisted upon. They regressed in time to three teenagers, three children, two, then one – just Beatrice, chubby-cheeked and caught mid-laugh, between a youthful-looking Mother and Dad...

"I love that one! That was my first Christmas as a mother, you know."

Beatrice jumped. She had been so absorbed, peering into Mother's eyes in the photo, that she hadn't heard her mother come into the room. She'd begun to wonder if Mother had felt anything like the fear she experienced when first she'd realized what was awaiting her. But now, Beatrice simply turned and was enveloped in an embrace that felt as reassuring as it had when she was a tiny child.

She awoke to the familiar sick feeling that she got nowadays when she went too long without eating. For a moment, she forgot where she was and reached for the lamp, only to find none there. Eventually she discovered a light switch, her robe and slippers, and stumbled upstairs.

The curtains weren't drawn, and she could see the first hints of dawn in the sky. In the half-light, she made her way to the kitchen and settled at the table with a basket of rolls and a generous pat of butter and turned on the radio. Bing Crosby was singing "White Christmas". The song had made her a little sad as a girl, growing up with palm trees and the beach throughout the winter. She got up to look for some jam. After a few moments with her head in the refrigerator, she turned around to find Eva staring at her.

"*Mija*, what are you doing up?"

Beatrice replaced the jam jar like a kid caught with a hand in her Christmas stocking before time. "I – ah – woke up and I was hungry." Her eyes slid to the table where the basket of rolls sat, far emptier than when she'd found it.

Eva switched on the kitchen lights and looked Beatrice over. Beatrice felt as naked as when Eva had given her her evening bath some twenty years before.

"*¿Embarazada?*" – Eva seemed to be posing the question more to herself than to Beatrice.

Beatrice knew she had once known what the word meant. Feeling faint, she retraced her steps and sat down again. *Embarrassed? No... something embarrassing...* She looked up, astonished. *How could she know?* Her throat squeezed shut as Eva folded her in an embrace:

"*¡Mija!*"

Beatrice started to cry. All this last month she had held herself together, even on long-distance calls with Patrick, but she could no longer keep the avalanche of emotion in check. Fear and doubt and worry and frustration – about the baby, her parents, her life plans, Patrick – came gushing out.

She sat there, holding onto Eva's ample waist, crying until she was spent. Her eyes were hot and her nose dripping by the time Eva finally disentangled herself. She returned in an instant with a napkin and a glass of water. Beatrice dabbed at her face and Eva, with a pat on the shoulder, put the kettle on and bustled around the kitchen starting breakfast.

Beatrice hadn't realized that Uncle Jasper and Aunt Nicola were coming for dinner until an hour before, when Mother suggested she change into "something more festive" – by which she meant fancier. Although they only lived in uptown La Jolla, Beatrice's aunt and uncle rarely came for dinner. In fact, even growing up, she'd seen them less frequently than her cousins up on the Central Coast. Like 'Aunt' Liz, Jasper was actually Mother's cousin, but still had, to some extent, filled the place of an uncle in a family where Mother had been an only child and Dad one of just two kids.

They sat down after a slightly stilted cocktail hour, and Eva brought out the soup. Patrick was seated next to Beatrice; she clung to his hand for a moment under the table before she dared taste anything. Thankfully, since her uncanny intuition, Eva had been most considerate in not serving too many foods with overpowering scents or flavors – though when Mother specifically requested fish or bleu cheese, not even Eva could help Beatrice.

Silver candlesticks cast pools of fluttering light on the table, and a fire burned on the hearth. A record of Nat "King" Cole Christmas carols played in the background, and the decorated tree twinkled in a big front window. All was calm and bright until Beatrice turned her attention back to the conversation. Aunt Nicola, her poison-red nails gleaming as she gestured, was enumerating the various evils of their neighbors' dog and virtues of their own little ball of fur – a canine so small it barely escaped classification as a rodent.

"You know," she said, leaning in with a conspiratorial air, "he barks all day long because they just *leave* him there. The wife works too," she added, with a half eye-roll aimed at Mother, who was presumably meant to agree that this was a fate worse than death.

Beatrice took a deep breath and smiled tightly. She sipped at wine she had not asked for. Her brothers were talking with Patrick about a new favorite surf spot, and Dad had started telling Uncle Jasper about how business had been in the past year. Beatrice knew it was silly to let her aunt's pettiness irritate her so and allowed herself to be distracted by arrival of the next course.

The soup had somehow made her hungrier; now it was lamb with all the trimmings. For a few blessed minutes there was no conversation but what pertained to refilling glasses, passing mint jelly or complimenting the food. The topic for moral inspection then turned to education.

Aunt Nicola and Uncle Jasper were impressed that Patrick was a professor. Beatrice stopped listening to the words being said and instead wondered how two people could be as different as Mother and Uncle Jasper, when they had spent so much time together as children. She knew it was a point of pain and disappointment to Mother that they saw so little of him now, so there must have been a better relationship back then, or at least hope of one. Beatrice hated to think that she could ever be on such chilly terms with her brothers.

Eva was clearing plates when Aunt Nicola's voice broke through the protective shell Beatrice had formed for herself:

"I don't see why you think something needs to change, Patrick. They don't need a college education to cook and clean, or garden or wait tables. Why give them ambitions beyond their station?"

"Nicola!" Mother exclaimed softly but firmly, "*Please!*" She looked meaningfully in Eva's direction as she returned to the kitchen with laden arms.

Nicola waved a dismissive hand, on which a chunky diamond refracted the candle-light: "You worry too much about her feelings, Jean. Anyway, it's not her job to listen to our conversation."

Beatrice found she was gripping Patrick's hand again under the table. He winced slightly but did not pull away.

*

"It's good to see you've found a man who loves you," Grandmother said, patting Beatrice's hand and beaming at the two of them.

Beatrice felt her heart clench, but tried not to alter the pressure with which she held Patrick's hand. Through all the phases of their arguably young and dramatic relationship, *that* word had hovered just outside, waiting to be invited in. Sometimes when he was bidding her goodnight on the phone he would say, "Goodnight, my love." Did that count? Beatrice had worked up the courage to tell him she was pregnant, but she had not yet found the courage to face the question within: Did she *love* him? the man she was now legally bound to "Till death us do part"?

What if (she tried to avoid the thought whenever possible) she had the leaving gene, like Grandmother? In fairness, Grandmother had only left two *actual* husbands and one engagement; another had died – and a person couldn't control for that, barring murder. Mother and Dad had always spoken in subdued tones about her latest husband-to-be, which only heightened a young Beatrice's curiosity. The impressive array of suitors and husbands had been in the background all through her early years. Grandmother had always seemed happiest near the start of a relationship, a pattern Beatrice had come to recognize only as she herself approached adulthood and contemplated the uncharted territory of romance.

The boat captain had been her personal favorite, although the Austrian nobleman whom Grandmother was currently seeing was certainly handsome (also a fair bit younger than her), and his stories of the homeland – if they were to be credited – were a source of considerable fascination. But was this proclivity of Grandmother's to serial relations a gene one could inherit? Was there perhaps an official term that could make it sound more respectable than "a wandering eye" – hopefully nothing too Freudian?

In all fairness, Beatrice had never heard her grandmother's side of the story about her series of men. Maybe there was a perfectly good reason behind each broken promise, and therefore Beatrice had nothing to fear. Certainly Mother appeared as devoted to Dad as ever, and vice versa...

Beatrice sat in an over-exposed room, flicking through pages of last September's *Vogue*. She glanced (again) at a large – it must be life-sized – model of a woman's torso, the stomach swollen as in late pregnancy and cross-sectioned to show more of the female anatomy than Beatrice recalled learning about in school. Nested within the faceless figure, head downward (which surprised her), was what looked like a baby doll. She'd seen those photographs in *Life* as a teenager – infants as they looked *in utero*. This chunky model baby with plastic eyes closed looked nothing like they had – almost ethereal, reminding her of images of nebulae in far galaxies.

Her own idea of the baby growing inside her was even more nebulous. Some days, she pictured it fully formed as (all going well) she would hold him or her in her arms some months hence; it favored Patrick when it came to features, but had her eyes. At other times, she thought of it more like some alien invader; still others, she wondered whether it was really there at all. Then the midwifery nurse walked in, and Patrick laid his hand on Beatrice's shoulder, and she remembered that she was scared, but not alone.

The nurse squeezed a blob of blue goop onto her stomach. Beatrice caught her breath at how cold it was. Then the nurse began moving a gray wand around on her abdomen, where it was starting to look like she'd had several large meals back to back. Beatrice was so intent on watching what the nurse was doing that she forgot about the screen until the nurse pointed up at it to say: "There's your baby. Measuring right on schedule!" – She beamed at Beatrice and Patrick as though they knew just what she was talking about.

Beatrice held Patrick's hand tightly, staring at the grainy charcoal image, wondering if it was indeed obvious where the baby was. She glanced at him; his expression was blank. Finally, the nurse smiled again and, using her free hand, pointed out the little head – and from there a little bud of a human began taking shape on the monitor and in Beatrice's mind. The heartbeat they saw too, so much faster than hers, but sustained quite literally by her own heart.

It was after her ultrasound that Beatrice began having flashbacks... A young Beatrice heard a noise from the living room and quietly poked her head into her parents' bedroom. Mother and Dad were standing near the French doors that led onto the balcony; morning light fell on their bent heads. Dad was near Mother, hand on her shoulder. They were absorbed by what was cupped in Mother's hand. Beatrice peered at it:

In a puddle of blood and fluid lay a small, curving form that Beatrice slowly recognized from diagrams she'd seen with Mother during visits to the OB/GYN for her previous pregnancies. Meanwhile, Mother said something in a mournful tone, Beatrice was sure, but it was hard to recall. The image was blurred and crumpled at the edges, like a photograph after too much handling. Her parents had stood there together, and she had quietly slipped back downstairs to her bedroom to cry.

Beatrice now could not be sure whether the terror that gripped her some nights was to do with a memory of her mother's pain, or if the sonogram image had done something to make her feel more connected to the child inside her.

The absolute quiet of snow! She had already forgotten it, the way it could muffle sound and make you feel as if you were the only beings left in the universe – though not in a terrifying, existential way; it was like being wrapped in a comforter of absolute white. She tried to let the peacefulness wash over her. They had come back to the cabin with Patrick's parents for a long weekend, in order to tell them the baby news. She hadn't seen them since Thanksgiving; Patrick had been forced to deliver their elopement news alone while she was in bed with a bad cold at New Year's.

No doubt the Woodings would think her a complete tramp when they found out about the pregnancy. Beatrice's stomach knotted itself and she clutched fistfuls of the overlong sleeves she was wearing. She'd put on one of Patrick's sweaters the previous night and this morning to conceal the news before they had a chance to tell his family.

Patrick had been in favor of revealing everything at once – marriage, baby, all of it – but Beatrice had argued that that was nigh on heart-attack inducing. In truth, she'd wanted to put off the inevitable as long as possible. They had not yet told her family about the baby either. Glancing through the big picture windows, she saw her in-laws now up and stirring, and turned to go back inside.

Patrick's dad built a fire in the wood-burning stove. It was cozy at first but soon began to feel suffocating. Maybe it was Patrick's cable-knit pullover that made Beatrice so hot; no one else seemed to be sweating. Patrick's mother brought out coffee in earthenware mugs. Beatrice smiled and set hers down as soon as she judged polite. She was still not able to stomach coffee, even as many of her other aversions were beginning to subside.

She felt like a frog must feel in the proverbial pot of slowly heating water, right before it shuffles off this mortal coil. How on earth was she supposed to be strong and face whatever came next when she felt like this? Patrick, seated beside her on the love seat, was talking football with his dad and hadn't noticed her tugging at the neck of the sweater or shoving back her sleeves. At length, conversation died away.

Beatrice struggled with a mouthful of coffee.

"Ready, honey?" – Patrick placed his palm on her thigh.

All at once Beatrice knew with horror what she was ready for and, setting down her mug and moving his hand as calmly as possible, sprinted for the guest bathroom. Clearly everyone could hear exactly what happened next, because Patrick arrived a minute later with a damp washcloth to wipe the sweat from her neck and a toothbrush and toothpaste to help her mouth taste less vile.

She had a sudden, almost physical need to tell him that she loved him, but her stomach was still unsteady, so she contented herself with squeezing his right hand, as with his left he continued dabbing at her temples.

Minutes later, they emerged together.

"Are you okay?" – Mrs. Wooding looked concerned. "Do you want to lie down? Patrick, get her some water."

"I'll be all right, thanks." – Beatrice sipped the water cautiously, relieved that she need not face coffee again.

Mrs. Wooding held her head to one side, observing them both. "Ahh," she said after a moment, "I believe I may have a guess about what you wanted to tell us."

"Tell us? What? Paula, what's going on?" – Patrick's father looked from his wife to them and back.

"If I'm not mistaken, my dear, we're going to be grandparents again!"

Decisions, Beatrice thought, so rarely happen all at once. More often, they come in fragments and, over time, we sift through and piece them together, till at last we come to a "point of decision" when we choose the thing we've been moving towards and puzzling out all along. Occasionally, though, the press of circumstances forces our hand, and only after the choice is made are we afforded a full opportunity to reflect on whether it was, in fact, the right decision.

Beatrice had watched Patrick shake his father's hand when they'd arrived, kiss his mother's cheek, tousle the head of the dog, all with unfeigned affection, and she had tallied those in the 'right choice' column. She recalled him cursing at a driver who had pulled out in front of them on the journey up to the cabin, which made her wonder if he would control his temper when she or their baby tested its limits. She told herself that she would never have had so many questions and doubts if they were only dating. But they were *not*.

She remembered perfectly the first time she'd read *Little Women*, because that was the first time she'd fallen in love. Theodore Laurence (aka Laurie or Teddy) had stolen her heart as completely as only a young girl's heart can be stolen – perhaps more so since he was a fictional character, and thus immune to the less romantic traits of living, breathing males, including but not limited to a tendency to find bodily functions amusing. Beatrice had been heartbroken when Jo refused Laurie's proposal, knowing that she herself would never have been so foolish, and she had barely been able to forgive Jo by the end of the book.

From Laurie it was a natural progression to Mr. Knightley, Captain Wentworth and (of course) Mr. Darcy. The vibrancy of Beatrice's literary romantic adventures had almost made up for the lack of real-life suitors. Her native shyness, for which her brothers had often teased her, as well as a notable lack of boys at The Bishop's School until her high school years, had not helped matters.

The first few times a guy had asked her out, Beatrice had been so taken aback at how different he was from her ideals that she'd declined almost without registering the offer. To her mind, this was simply not how it should be. By the time she got to college, she was starting to be concerned – most men were far more average than she'd hoped. Her friends smiled indulgently as she described her perfect suitor: strong yet sensitive; artistic yet masculine; witty, good humored yet occasionally brooding; tall, dark and handsome, obviously.

Those college friends had been no help. Louisa, who'd been in modeling shoots practically since infancy, would toss her perfect curls and say that men were far less civilized than Beatrice imagined, but far easier to tame. "You just have to learn to play the game, Bea!"

Hannah, meanwhile, was hopelessly in love with Stewart, who, Beatrice could tell, was only riding that wave till a better one came along. Hannah's blindness in fact terrified Beatrice as much as Louisa's coolly calculated methods put her off.

Everyone acknowledged that Beatrice's own parents' love story was out of a fairy tale, but that did little to help.

Then one day she was reading in Jeremiah how God declared his love for his people – "I have loved you with an everlasting love; therefore I have continued my faithfulness to you" – and she thought, *perhaps here is a love to render all other loves unnecessary.* Truth be told, there seemed a certain safety in a life such as that of a nun, where one had only to love God, family and one's fellow nuns and need never really deal with the male of the species.

Beatrice watched a hawk being chased off by three crows, soaring on its more powerful wings while they flapped and cawed frantically. They were defending their nests, she knew, but she empathized with the larger, graceful bird of prey. Did that make her a bad mother-to-be?

She sometimes felt that she witnessed private dramas in all sorts of places where others saw only randomness. A killdeer crying and feigning a broken wing, dragging itself across a freshly tilled field to draw attention away from its nest of brown-speckled eggs; a red-tailed hawk circling and diving and diving again, until it settled into the brush with a snake or gopher in its talons... Maybe other people's lives were like that: ciphers to all but those who knew what signs to look for. Why, when she could read the language of nature, and had been called a mind-reader by her friends, was Patrick sometimes so inscrutable to her? – It was as if his private thoughts and feelings were locked away in a vault, save when he deigned (or remembered) to invite her in. On the other hand, there were times when his thoughts were obvious, yet he seemed to think she wouldn't be able to see through the most evident subterfuge. Case in point: he'd bought her Christmas gift while they were out shopping, then made some feeble excuse about a bag from a jewelry store holding a gift for his grandmother...

They'd reached a stage beyond which Beatrice, for all her imagination, could imagine nothing. She had anticipated and dreaded this moment, and asked herself again and again what would happen after the words were finally said... They were sitting with Mother and Dad on the beach in front of the Walnut Lounge, everyone but Beatrice sipping a pre-dinner cocktail. She had lost her taste for alcohol as well as coffee since becoming pregnant, so she had opted instead for a Shirley Temple, which might have occasioned comment had her brothers been there.

Her parents, she knew, had put her weekend visit down to missing Patrick, but in reality Beatrice was at the point when she could conceal her pregnancy no longer. Both physically and emotionally, the truth was forcing itself into view. A winter sunset was flaming across the horizon when Patrick caught her eye and raised his brow. She nodded, swallowing what threatened at the back of her throat.

"Mr. and Mrs. Grey" – he persisted in addressing them formally, despite Mother in particular assuring him that he could call them by their Christian names – "Beatrice and I have some, ah, exciting news."

Beatrice studied her parents for indications that they had guessed. Both smiled blandly – apparently not. She wasn't sure: should she be happy that the thought hadn't crossed their minds yet?

"We're having a baby!" she blurted quickly, so that Patrick wouldn't have to.

"Darling – how wonderful!" Mother jumped up to embrace her and kiss her on the forehead. "You look so slim, I would never have guessed."

Dad shook Patrick's hand; he was still smiling, but said nothing. Then they traded places and he was folding her into a hug while Mother kissed Patrick on the cheek.

Everyone beamed as they settled back to their drinks, and Beatrice was almost ready to breathe a sigh of relief when she realized what no one had asked: when she was due.

It was getting dark by the time they went into the Club dining room for an early supper, but her appetite had gone.

*

With the progression of seasons and slow ballooning of her belly, Beatrice's anxiety about her qualifications for motherhood grew. She tried to remember what it had been like when her brother Tom was a baby – there was no chance she'd remember Will's infancy. But even Tom's babyhood eluded her; she had only been four, after all. What about babysitting? She had memories of watching a couple of bald, chunky infants when she was fourteen or so; they were the offspring of neighbors or family friends, and she'd felt quite calm caring for them. Yet now she just knew she would forget how to change a diaper, or let the baby's head fall back once and damage her child's spine forever! Perhaps the advantage of being a fourteen-year-old was that one didn't comprehend yet *all* the ways that life could go wrong, and therefore didn't spend much time speculating about potential calamities. And she hadn't been the parent in those cases, so she could adopt a more coolly rational perspective.

If reflecting on past experiences with children didn't do much to reassure her, Beatrice needed another strategy. At length she pulled out a sheaf of sheet music, which had languished in a cupboard since she'd discovered that she was to be a mother rather than a renowned composer or a nun. Although she had dreaded practicing often during her musical training, the sense of calm was almost immediate now as she settled into a Bach prelude to warm up her fingers. The Prelude in C was her favorite, recognizable to most since Gounod had adapted it for his *Ave Maria*.

Meanwhile, the rains came steadily for California that year. A week or two of sunshine was followed by a good rain, and green crept up and up the rough brown mountainsides. The hills lit up in spring the way a woman lights up at the sight of the one she loves, or a piece of paper suddenly blooms with flame on the hearth. The mustard appeared at first as the faintest glimmer of yellow – you almost weren't sure it was there. Then it spread like a tide across the valleys and over the flanks of the now-green foothills.

There were other signs of life, too. Poppies laughed at the sun from the roadside; tiny rabbits appeared at dawn and dusk, hopping about among the larger cottontails in gardens and on lawns; and Beatrice's own body began to awaken in strange new ways. Then, one day in mid-March, she was standing at the sink doing the dishes when she froze, the dishcloth halfway into a water-glass. She had the oddest impression that there was something inside her tapping politely to get out. Then she remembered that there *was* someone inside her, and her mouth dropped open as she realized she'd felt the baby move for the first time.

Stillness descended over her, like the descending of a dove. It wasn't that everything grew quiet: she could still hear the same sounds and feel the same sensations. But suddenly there was time for each: a bird chirping unseen by the kitchen window, the failing light of the sun beyond the pines, a candle's warm flicker, the beat of her own heart. Beatrice breathed them all in, and slowly exhaled. She almost expected this peace to dissipate like mist, but it remained. It was an underground river, steadily flowing, into which she had only now delved deep enough to discover.

My dear Beatrice,

It sounds as if you have reached one of those seasons of life where, after a long period of relative sameness, big events pile on top of each other. I know you, my friend, despite the miles and long periods of separation between us. Now is not time for self-recrimination, but to face your future boldly, with the confidence that, if this new life was entrusted to you, you will find in your faith, yourself, your husband and your community, the strength to raise this child well.

'Be it unto me according to thy word,' is one of the simplest and hardest things we are ever called to say to God. He is the one who chooses the life to which he calls each of us. The great discipline is but to say "yes" when the time comes...

Beatrice nodded mutely as she read, feeling any moment she might dissolve in tears of mingled disappointment and relief. She was unlikely ever to reach the heights of dedication to her art (and certainly not to a religious order) to which she'd aspired, but there was comfort in the knowledge that God saw this as a good life too – one that, for whatever reason, she'd long felt compelled to sacrifice in pursuit of some higher good. It was time to get on with the life she had, instead of dreaming of other lives she might be living.

Anna's letter went on to laud the power of attending to simple graces and small pleasures, as a way to recognize life's inherent beauty. Beatrice liked that idea and began making a mental list as she folded clothes or swept floors or made the bed: the cool breezes that washed over their coastal community even in summer; a smell of eucalyptus after rain; the songs of blackbirds in mustard – perched precariously or darting suddenly, orange patches on the wings of the males flaming in flight; that delicious weariness after hours spent at sun-soaked beaches – a million accumulated small gifts, *showings*, that she was so apt to take for granted...

For the first time, she thought about Patrick as father of their child – not as an abstract mental exercise, but in fact. They were painting the baby's crib, a hand-me-down from his sister Beth, on their new back patio. Beatrice had put off giving up her room in a bungalow on Chorro Street because it had felt like, so long as they weren't living together, there was a way out and she could pretend she wasn't really married to a man that she'd known for less than a year. At last, however, he'd forestalled her argument against moving back to La Jolla by landing this guest lecturer position at Cal Poly. He had driven up the coast to tell her the news and scheduled several rental viewings for the same weekend. Before Beatrice was able to concoct another objection, she'd found herself falling in love with a Craftsman cottage on Garden Street, with a stained-glass pane in the front door and a gnarled lemon tree in the back yard. And now they were kneeling on newspapers on the bricked-over portion of that yard, painting the crib.

Once they'd moved in together, Beatrice saw that Patrick had begun to recognize all her stalling for what it was. It pained her to think how the realization must hurt him. He didn't need to remind her that she could have refused his proposal, even though the life of a single mother and, more importantly, of a child born out of wedlock did not seem like a choice. After all, she told herself, he *had* moved to a town he barely knew for her sake. And she *had* begun to fall in love with him before everything had started happening too fast.

She was trying to overcome her doubts sufficiently to make him feel at home. She'd made a couple of passable dinners, which they ate together politely at their new dining-room table. He bought her flowers on his cycle home from campus one day, but she got stuck on how to respond and somehow ended up giving him a grandmotherly peck on the cheek. Needless to say, as he divined her unease at their situation, he didn't so much as touch her hand when they went to bed. Yet now, perhaps for the first time since their marriage, as they worked on something to hold *their* sleeping child, Beatrice felt herself relaxing into the easy camaraderie they'd shared in the beginning.

Patrick gestured dramatically with his paintbrush while quoting e. e. cummings, flicking robin's egg blue onto bricks.

"Well, that defeats the point of newspaper, doesn't it?" she laughed, and he ducked into the kitchen for a bucket of soapy water and a rag.

She moved to stand up, and one of those spasms the nurse had called Braxton Hicks caught her breath. Patrick dropped the rag and kicked over the bucket as he ran back to her. There was no hesitation this time; he took her hand in his and placed his other hand on her back.

"What's wrong? What do you need?"

She looked into his eyes and knew that, though he left the toilet seat up too often and had yet to take out the trash without her asking, he would be a good father. A good husband too, she suspected, if she let him, but she would reserve her judgement on that a bit longer.

Life felt like a juggling act for which she had not been trained. Beatrice recalled wistfully the adult existence she'd imagined for herself as a girl: living in a castle in England, meeting and swiftly marrying a count, balls and horse-riding and of course lots of big, swishy dresses. In her imagination, love had been a given, though she didn't yet know what it felt like outside of books or how it would lead to the eight children she planned on to populate her castle (along with a generous number of dogs). Love then had seemed tied to the scenic backdrops against which she set these adventures. She and her count would gaze longingly at one another across a wild moor, or dance on a star-canopied terrace overlooking a loch or ride along a lonely beach where crystalline waves made the only sound aside from their horses' hooves. Once in a while she'd try putting a poem into the count's mouth, which he would recite by heart from below her casement window.

Had she mistaken the lovely for love? She certainly thrilled to hear Patrick declaim a bit of John Donne, but what more often filled her with a crown-to-toes flood of emotion was simpler. A cup of something hot while watching the sun rise from Terrace Hill, him telling her he'd missed her when she was away for a night visiting an old friend, him doing the dishes after dinner when her back pain began to increase in early summer...

Love, she decided one Saturday afternoon while ironing nursery curtains, had a lot to do with presence. Not that you couldn't be away from someone and still love them, but there was something irreplaceable about coming home sweaty and flustered after an exhausting search for baby-sized bed linens to find that your husband had been to the deli for rotisserie chicken and coleslaw so you didn't have to think about cooking. Beatrice almost turned to putty when Patrick helped her take off the shoes that were now too tight and then massaged her feet. He caught her looking at him where he sat on the shaggy mustard carpet. She felt naked as neither of them looked away, and her eyes filled with tears – tears of gratitude for what he was doing, but also of hope, because she was beginning to feel that maybe they could do this together. One tear rolled along her nose and plopped onto her overalls, which she'd begun to wear like a uniform. A second one followed along her cheek. He reached up and brushed it away with his thumb. On impulse she grabbed his hand and pulled him toward her. He looked like a scared child for a moment, all defenses down, and her heart yearned toward him even more.

Beatrice lay in bed, Patrick breathing steadily beside her. Her body was so tired she felt like crying, if only it didn't take so much effort. She'd gone to bed exhausted, yet after only a couple of blissful hours of sleep, she was stuck here once more, staring into the dark and trying not to resent *him* for getting a solid eight hours every damn night.

She'd tried tricking her body back to sleep with the usual: warm milk, a textbook on linguistics, then counting sheep. She could have screamed in frustration; nothing worked.

Finally, she took to starting down a trail of thought, trying to let her mind associate freely and directing her thoughts as little as possible. Perhaps this way she could get her brain to finally let go, and she'd drift off to delicious slumber.

She found herself remembering a drive she'd taken many months before when the hills were still verdant and grapes freshly pruned. She'd stopped to look at the bereft-looking vines: there remained only the barest scaffolding of what they would be in summer and fall; they seemed humbled after their late autumn glory of red and gold. Beatrice had felt a kinship with those close-cut vines, and now more than ever. Her life was being pruned on all sides. Less than a year before, she had had all manner of shoots and tendrils and leaves. Now possibility after possibility was being lopped off. She knew what remained would blossom in its own way, but she had not chosen her path freely, and it stung.

What also smarted were the glances longtime neighbors and acquaintances had given her budding stomach the last time she and Patrick had visited La Jolla. It seemed to her that they would have forgiven her any number of affairs, but the idea that she must have gotten pregnant before the wedding was somehow beyond the pale. Beatrice felt drained of charity: she had no patience for these people and their shallow lives. After all, she remembered how some of them had comported themselves when they thought no one was looking. There had been that wilder than average party at her parents' house, back when she was a teenager...

She'd arrived home to find the doors and windows all open and light, people and music spilling out onto the drive. She thought it was Coltrane playing – her parents loved jazz. A general sound of laughter and good cheer filled the air, along with summer scents of jasmine and gardenia. Beatrice wasn't usually home for these parties. She and her siblings were given permission to spend the night at friends' houses, and that was generally an arrangement pleasing to all.

That night, though, Beatrice's friend Linda Lightfoot had snuck out for a date, leaving her alone in a cavernous house with an unsettling painting of cats and dogs in business suits staring at her from across the living room. Linda's parents had at the last moment announced they were going for cocktails with Mr. Lightfoot's business partner; Cook would make the girls dinner, and they'd be back before late. *They* might be, but Beatrice doubted that Linda would.

In junior high years, Linda and Beatrice had been inseparable, but since starting high school, things had felt different. Beatrice had attributed it to their more rigorous academic schedule, but tonight as she'd sat on the Lightfoots' ivory sofa alone, she thought perhaps she'd been naïve. Maybe she didn't see more of Linda because she was simply no longer a priority to her; boys and clothes and slimming diets were all Linda had wanted to talk about as she did her hair and makeup. She told Beatrice she was a pal for not tattling on her before Beatrice had been given a choice in the matter. Then a car had squealed to the curb and Linda ran out, draping a coat loosely over her bare shoulders.

The boy at the wheel had looked old enough to be a senior, and Beatrice wondered, as she waved goodbye from the deck, how Linda had planned to slip away if her parents had not so obligingly waltzed out themselves. Then she collected her things to walk the few blocks home. She would rat on no one, but Linda could explain herself as she liked to her parents upon their, or her, return.

Once Beatrice saw the extent of the party her parents were throwing, she began to question whether she could cozy up in bed with a book without anyone noticing, as she'd intended. At the same time, she felt an electric charge in the air – perhaps exhilaration of the unknown or celebratory energy suffusing the atmosphere.

She left the steep, ivy-lined front drive to enter through a back door on the lower level, which gave onto the lawn. The music was louder inside even this far from the epicenter, which she took to be the bar upstairs. Beatrice allowed herself to entertain the daring and improbable thought of changing into her most adult-looking dress, putting her hair up and slipping upstairs for a closer look. She might even grab a martini from the bar, just to blend in.

Rounding the corner to her room without encountering anyone, she hadn't yet had time to breathe a sigh of relief when she opened her door and stopped, barely able to believe her eyes. A couple sat on *her* bed, locked in a sweaty embrace. Two half-drunk martinis sat on her nightstand, and a tie and a pair of stilettos lay on the floor. Mercifully, neither of the faces became visible before Beatrice slammed the door in a panic and retreated down the hall.

She felt queasy, her clenched fists damp with sweat. For a moment she could hear nothing, only the pounding of her heart in her ears. Then the music drifted back in: "Only You" by The Platters; then, a sound of nearby voices – *theirs.*

"Who was that?" – A woman's tone. "Who *was* that?!"

"Not sure..." The man's voice, and, to Beatice's horror, one that she recognized.

"Darling, see if you can persuade whoever it is not to say anything, won't you?"

Beatrice heard someone get up and realized she was about to come face to face with some man she knew, who had been busy sticking his tongue down a woman's throat in *her* room. She darted down the rest of the hallway and into the library, pulling the door nearly shut behind her.

Her heart was beating a quick staccato now. She was sure they could hear her breathing from the other room. She saw her bedroom door open a crack and stay that way. They must be looking for her, or checking that the coast was clear. After a moment, a distinguished-looking man with graying hair emerged to stare down the hallway. Beatrice shrank back, hoping that the darkness of the library would protect her sliver of face from his view.

In the event he apparently did not notice her, because after a glance in the opposite direction he turned his back to Beatrice, and the woman emerged. Mrs. De Soto, Mother's friend from the Las Patronas committee! Her voluptuous curves and signature blood-red lipstick had long been objects of envy among Beatrice and her flat-chested friends, whose parents did not yet allow them to wear makeup. Now the lipstick had formed something of a corona around Mrs. De Soto's mouth, and her hair was cascading out from its usual twist – but it was her. And that was *certainly* not her husband, though Beatrice hadn't gotten a good enough look at him to know who he was. She knew that voice though...

The pair moved out of sight, and Beatrice was left in a quandary: slip down the hallway once more to her own room and try to sleep, despite the fact that her bed had been so casually violated; or, stay here in the library till the party was over. She skipped quickly over her earlier fantasy of mingling with the guests incognito; it no longer held any appeal.

Switching on a table lamp, she picked up the book lying beside it: *The Scarlet Pimpernel*. She slouched back in a worn leather chair and began to read. The pages and minutes bled swiftly together as she began to wander, entranced, through England and France of the 1790s. The swashbuckling exploits, clever disguises and hairbreadth escapes enchanted her, as did the otherworldly life of European nobility. Yet without doubt it was the Scarlet Pimpernel himself and his romance with Marguerite St. Just that captivated her most: such passionate intensity was alarming but deeply attractive. Then, somewhere in the midst of Lord Grenville's ball, weariness and another kind of exhaustion from her tumultuous evening overcame her, and Beatrice fell asleep...

She awoke to her father's hand on her shoulder. She jumped, and her book slid off her lap. She had just been dreaming she was an aristocrat in disguise, trying to escape Paris before she was discovered and taken to Madame la Guillotine, and for a second the hand on her shoulder was that of a French revolutionary soldier about to seize her. Dad's face was a most welcome replacement, however puzzled he seemed. The watery light of early morning was streaming through the open door behind him.

"Beatrice, what are you doing here? We thought you were staying at Linda's." – After a moment's thought, he added, "Why aren't you in your own bed?"

Beatrice took a minute to register surprise that no one at Linda's house had even reported her absence, before she realized in a panic that she had to come up with an explanation for her choice of sleeping quarters. She opened her mouth to tell a white lie to spare everyone's feelings, but

Dad's look of concern, coupled with the unsettling events of last night, were too much for her, and she burst into tears.

*

She was beginning to understand that all truly important things in life took time. For most of her existence, waiting had rankled her, but she saw a peculiar beauty in it now. Waiting was the outworking of a patience born of love. One only waited, hoping against hope, for things that one valued deeply. Mothers, like her, waited expectantly for their babies to enter the world; lovers waited for their affections to be returned (sometimes a very long time); God waited for humans to love him – the most beautiful waiting of all. But such waiting was not passive. Her body was working tirelessly (not without cost) to nurture this baby; a lover wooed, whether by poems and flowers, or, more to her taste, wine and lots of hikes in the mountains; God incarnated himself, ultimately in his Son but also in everyday advents – a blade of grass beaded with dew, a newborn lamb's tiny bleat. God waits for us, and often for long periods we do not know it. T. S. Eliot had, unsurprisingly, put his finger on it: "The faith and the love are all in the waiting."

She laid her palm softly on her abdomen: "I hope you know how much I love you. I've been waiting two thirds of a year to meet you, after all!"

Patrick flipped through a scrapbook of recipe cuttings, some dotted with sauce, others heavily annotated, still others already becoming crusty with age.

"Your mom saved *all* of these? Did she make them all?"

"I don't know. How could I know that, Patrick?"

He stopped turning the pages and looked up. "I thought maybe these were her 'tried and true' recipes or something." – His tone was carefully even, and Beatrice realized how petulant her reply had sounded.

"I'm sorry, Patrick. It's just that – I'll never be the domestic goddess my mother is – especially not when my ankles are the size of my thighs and my stomach is the size of –" she looked around, lacking a ready metaphor, "of an armchair!"

He put down the book and came over, wrapping his arms around her and the eight-to-nine months watermelon (or armchair) that had once been her stomach. "You know, Beatrice, you haven't considered the fact that I might be a domestic god. You haven't really given me the chance to display my culinary accomplishments."

Tears burned into her eyes. Damn these pregnancy hormones! "But Patrick, you work all day, and I –"

"Your body is working all day and all night, growing a new human being. Honestly, seeing as you're a modern woman, I'm disappointed this wasn't your idea!"

Beatrice felt her mouth go slack. She watched as, after dropping a kiss on her forehead, Patrick donned one of her floral and gingham aprons (a gift from Great-Aunt Ida) and began flipping back through the recipes with renewed purpose, whistling as he did. If she hadn't been so tired that her body felt twice its usual pregnancy weight, she would have flung herself on top of him right there in the living room with the curtains open to the street.

"I was worried I'd be a bad mother too." Mother smiled sadly as if she'd read Beatrice's thoughts for nine months.

Now that it was time for the baby to appear, fear was once again Beatrice's frequent companion. But Mother, surely – "You were?"

"Yes. And with more reason."

Mother blinked back tears and Beatrice, after a moment's surprise, laid a hand on her forearm. They watched the shadows of sago palm fronds bob up and down the bricks in a light wind. After a moment, Mother cleared her throat and dabbed at her face with her handkerchief.

"My mother tried, once, to explain to me why she needed her freedom. And I daresay if it had been a friend telling me why she had to leave the raising of her daughter to her own parents and a maiden sister, I might have understood, in a way. But when your own mother tells you she could not bear the constraints of traditional womanhood – well, it's hard not to believe that in some way you are the problem."

She forestalled Beatrice's protest: "Oh, I know that's not what she meant! The explanation came at a time when she must have thought I was mature enough to understand – but still I spent years wondering why, if my mother loved me as she said she did, she didn't want to be around all of the time, like other girls' mothers."

Beatrice felt scalding tears sliding down her cheeks.

"So yes, I worried I would be a bad mother, because I only had an example of the parent I did *not* want to be. Though I vowed not to, I worried that somehow I'd still end up being exactly like my mother…

"Now I see that your grandmother did what she did to survive a desiccated marriage. And I see that same iron strength of conviction in you, although I know you'll channel it very differently."

They sat in silence for a time, listening to a bird warble from a neighbor's garden, then watching it flit into their lemon tree. Beatrice thought it might be some variety of gold-finch – she'd been dabbling in bird-watching lately. Whatever it was, this fellow sounded like it was bursting with gladness to be alive.

"Is it worth it?" she asked her mother finally. "Is it worth it, loving a man?"

Mother's look was a mix of amusement and compassion.

She said, finally: "From the moment I met your father, I had little choice in the matter, though I wasn't so honest with myself then. He *happened* to me, and my life was forever altered. I suppose later on one *chooses* to carry on loving in times of – difficulty..." Their eyes met. After a pause, Mother continued, "But I don't know how things are between you and Patrick."

Beatrice flushed: so many unspoken things. She suspected Mother had intuited most of the truth, just as she herself had, all those years ago, after that terrible party.

"All I can say is, if I could do it again, there's no one with whom I would rather have shared my life. If you can say that about Patrick, at least so far... well, you'll be all right."

Beatrice sucked in her breath. She felt a rush of warmth between her legs and looked down to see a growing patch of dark blue on her light-wash overalls. She began to blush again, but Mother said briskly:

"Well, it looks like it's time! Let's call Patrick."

Panic clutched at Beatrice as she realized she had *not* wet herself. This was the beginning of labor, the end result of which would be a new person who would alter the course of their lives forever – who had, in fact, already begun to do so.

*

The wine-dark scent of fallen apples, fermenting in golden days of October fog and sun – you could get drunk off the smell. The whole world felt more alive than it had in the hot, sleepy September just past. Every year Beatrice felt she had discovered life all over again in October, but never more so than this fall.

Poison oak crept up the wooded hillside like a vein of fire, its flame-gilded leaves almost making her forget its noxious nature. Snowberries flourished amid the undergrowth, plants with clusters of plump white fruit in sharp relief against their darker surroundings. Birds sang with abandon in the apple orchard across the road where, in addition to fragrant apples on the ground, she could see others blushing on boughs.

A small noise from the stroller called her attention back, and she bent forward and peaked beneath the awning. Peachy cheeks and blue eyes, wide as if they'd seen the whole of the universe before landing here on earth, greeted her.

"Hello Elena," She whispered.

She didn't know why she whispered, since her daughter was already awake. Beatrice still felt awe in the presence of this new life, awe that had first confronted her at the moment of giving birth, but was also familiar. She'd felt a faint echo of it before, as she'd watched a calf being born at her cousins' farm. The source of the awe was hard to pinpoint, but it had to do with a feeling that Elena was privy to some secret of existence that grown-ups had long since forgotten.

Beatrice had heard from Mother that when you had a child it was as if your heart were beating outside of your body. Beatrice had always taken this to mean that you were doubly vulnerable. But now, staring down in wonder at the tiny face poking out of the blankets, eyes blinking at the light and one long-fingered hand clutching a fold of fabric with surprising ferocity, she knew that Mother's words were more than a warning or a clever expression. That was actually how it felt: as if her heart had sprouted feet and walked out of her body and into the body of their child. It was a terrifying, electrifying, glorious feeling – a kind of falling in love that Beatrice had neither wanted nor knew now how to resist.

She looked at her watch. Probably time to be getting back. Patrick would be home soon from teaching, and he was as much enthralled by their offspring as she, eager not to miss a single, microscopic development. Later that night, once he and the baby were both asleep, she could write to Anna about a thought that had been percolating in her mind on her walk, an aspiration she hoped would become a lodestar for her life:

I never want to be lulled again into believing there's such a thing as an ordinary day. I never again want to experience life as anything other than a continuous, startling miracle, an unpredictable adventure that defies categorization.

***

Made in the USA
Monee, IL
02 June 2023

34731285R00090